Corliss

And Other Award-Winning Stories

Heather Haven

The Wives of Bath Press

www.thewivesofbath.com

The Wives of Bath Press
5512 Cribari Bend
San Jose, Ca 95135

http:// www.thewivesofbath.com

Cover Art by Suzannah Safi
Edited by Baird Nuckolls
Layout and book production by
Heather Haven and Baird Nuckolls

Print ISBN: 978-0-9994584-1-9
eBook ISBN: 978-0-9994584-0-2

Corliss and Other Award Winning Stories
Blurb

I've always liked short stories, short shorts, and flash fiction. The investment of time is on the briefer side, and often just as rewarding as a novel. I've penned a few, myself, and selected my personal favorites, including a couple of flashes. All the selections involve murder, suspense, surprise or chicanery.
Some stories have pretty unlikely heroes, such as an English bulldog named Jemma. Some learn and grow, some go to jail, some die, some profit from other people's villainy. The common thread is their humanness, even the dog's.
I hope you enjoy reading these stories as much as I enjoyed writing them.

Previously published or contest winners:
Corliss – Dan Poynter's Global Ebook Awards 2013
Dental Plan – Book Breeze Magazine 2013
Socks – Wayne C. Long Short Stories 2011
Boo – MuseItup Publications - 2011
Jemma and the Shoe – The Armchair Aesthete – 2009

Dedication

This collection of short stories is dedicated to my mother, Mary Lee. No longer with us except in spirit and love, she was and is one of the guiding forces of my life. I also dedicate this book to my wonderful husband, Norman Meister, whose belief in me and love is a constant. You can't go wrong when wonderful people buoy you up in this life. I am a very blessed woman.

Acknowledgments

Despite what many people think, a writer's life is not a solitary one. At least mine isn't. Each story within this book has been work-shopped, critiqued, and bettered by the help of other writers. Without exception, my fellow writers have been generous with their comments, constructive criticism, and good will, as I have tried to be with them.

Much of this positive approach to one another's writing comes from writer and teacher, Ellen Sussman, with whom I had the good fortune to study for nearly six-years. During that time, my classmates and I learned many things, but the lesson I hold dearest is that the *work*, the words upon the paper, are more important than anything else. Consequently, feelings of insecurity, competitiveness, jealousy, or negativity are cast aside when the written word is paramount in our minds. No matter where I go in this life, I will always bless Ellen and her classes for stressing this approach and code of ethics.

Talent will out and many of my classmates have achieved success in the writing field. I want to thank them for helping me craft clearer and tighter stories. To name but a few and in no particular order they are, Tracy Guzeman, Catherine Latta, Jeff Monaghan, Shelly King, Maggie Wing, Bobbie Bermann, Sid Suri, Christine Chua, Barbara Olson, Mhaire Fraser, Eileen Bordy, Ana McCracken, Ellen O'Neil, Amy Ladd, Andrew Kloak, Monique Mulbry, Denise Sanford, Kathleen Courts, Patty Page, and Jocelyn Kelly. I know I've left someone out, so apologies upfront if your name is not here. Above all, I thank you!

I am also a member of a small writing group, consisting of Carter Schwonk, Myra Strober, and Jerry Berger, excellent writers all. They have given me great advice and support for the past three years. Thank you.

I would like to mention other authors I've met along the way, such as Meg Waite Clayton, Sheldon Siegel, Nancy J. Parra, Rebecca Dakhle, Vinnie Hansen, Roseanne Dowell, Ginger Jones Simpson, Camille Minichino, Cindy Sample, and Grace DeLuca. They share with others their knowledge, talents, business acumen, and love of what they do. Writing is a noble profession. I am proud to be a part of it, largely because of people like them.

Lastly, I could not leave the acknowledgement section of this book without mentioning a woman who is a writing buddy, business partner, editor, and friend: Baird Nuckolls. A superior writer, herself, she has a gift for asking just the right questions of a manuscript. Suggestions of 'opening up' a thought, a phrase, and even a character, often leads me to a richer, more developed story. Whenever I listen to her, my work becomes better. Thank you, Baird.

Dear Reader,

While I'm throwing out thanks here, thank you for taking the time to read some of my stories. If I had to pick a favorite, I don't think I could do it. They're like children to me. That's a writer for you.

If you have the time and inclination, please leave a review at **http://www.amazon.com/-/e/B004QL22UK** or dash me off an email at **heather@heatherhavenstories.com**. I would love to hear from you.

Once again, thank you for visiting the world of my imagination.

My best always,

Heather

Table of Contents

Corliss
A Short Story
by
Heather Haven

Corliss

Towns are a lot like people. Some good, some bad, but most a little of both. I expect if you talked to folks around here, they'd tell you Ash Flats is a good town. Twenty-five years ago, I was born here; I was raised here, and once, I killed a man here. But that's a secret between Robby and me. Ash Flats, Arkansas, population eight hundred and fifty-seven, probably holds a few secrets like that.

The town folk were friendly enough, but when I was growing up, we pretty much kept to ourselves. Grandma used to say that she didn't like to complain, but she'd never had a happy day in her life. She seemed to have a few good ones, though, especially when she'd take her Wild Turkey into the backyard and talk to the squirrels. She'd throw them walnuts and watch them go up and down that old black walnut tree, laughing her head off. She seemed happy enough then.

I was about fifteen when I met my mother. It was 1959, and she passed through on her way to Biloxi going to meet her new husband who got stationed there right after the hurricane.

Seeing her for the first time was a lot like looking in a mirror, only twenty years later on. We had the same long, red-brown, curly hair and what Grandma called "snappy green eyes." It all seemed to work better on my mother, though, because she had a bubbly personality, almost bubbling right out of the chair she sat in.

She seemed happy, too, my mother. Here she was, she said, thirty-six years old and finally married. And to a sergeant. She was going to have a fine life, she said, but he didn't know about me, and we were going to keep it that way. That was all right with me. I didn't know either of them, and what bad feelings I had about it passed that day when Grandma put her arms around me while we watched the back of my mother's car leave the driveway.

"She can't help it, Corliss," Grandma said, hugging me tight. "She never did have the sense God gave a lemon, my Jackie, even in the fifth grade. Copied the ingredients off the back of a Milky Way bar and tried to pass it off as a book report on the cocoa beans of Brazil. Met your daddy the week before he got sent to jail for robbing a gas station. They were a fine pair, your daddy and your momma. You're better off with me."

"I expect I am, Grandma."

"Try to look on the bright side of it."

"All right."

Then she ambled into the house, grabbed her Wild Turkey off the cracked, yellow top kitchen table, and went into the backyard to her squirrels.

I got to know Wayne the summer after I finished high school. Wayne was a lot older, maybe forty. I was never much at making friends, and that was about the time my best and only friend, Lanie Sue, got married and moved away. The year or two before when I'd walk back and forth to school, I'd seen Wayne watching me, standing in the door of the hardware store, his orange jacket saying "Wayne's Hardware," flapping in the breeze. Sometimes he'd wave. He never said anything to me, though, until that summer.

I'd gone into his store looking for a new spring for Grandma's back screen door. Wayne jumped all over it, saying I didn't know nothing about putting in a spring on the back door, a pretty little thing like me, and he'd better come over and do it. By then Grandma was pretty sick, staying in bed with her Wild Turkey, still talking to her squirrels, so when she died, I married Wayne. I guess you could say I looked on him like the daddy I never had.

That's not how he saw me, though. Our wedding night he came to me and said, "Now Corliss, I'm going to show you what a husband and wife do. I don't want you to be fearful."

"I won't be fearful, Wayne."

"You just relax, Corliss."

"All right."

Then he climbed on top of me and did his business, which was fine with me and over real quick. I had done the same thing once before with one of the Barker boys, didn't care for it much, and never did it again, no matter what Freddie Barker said. Or any of the other boys in school, neither.

Wayne was good to me, and I was sorry when he got hit by a truck eight months later in front of the store. I guess not everybody paid attention to that orange jacket. He was in the hospital for two days before he died. With me being a young widow, Wayne being gone sudden-like, and neither of us having any family, folks tried to be consoling.

They would drop by the house with casseroles, leaving them on the front porch, because I wouldn't come to the door when they rang the bell. You could say I was shy or in mourning, but with me growing up without a momma or daddy and a grandma who talked to squirrels, I stayed to myself a lot when I was a kid. I guess it just carried through into my womanhood. After a while, everybody got used to my ways.

So there I was, running a hardware store at the age of nineteen, wondering how to open the cash drawer, and hoping people would use those new things called credit cards so I wouldn't have to. The first week I wound up putting most of the cash I got under the straw decoration inside that old cracker barrel on display by the front door. By the end of the second week, I knew I had to start ordering supplies to replace what was flying out the door. When Robby walked in looking for a job, I was glad enough to give him one.

Short, thick, and hardly much taller than me, Robby had that kind of light blond, flyaway hair that looked like he put his finger in a light socket. He had those piercing blue eyes, too, the kind that try to see what's going on inside your soul. Sometimes you want to open up your chest, peel it off, and just hand it over to him. That's Robby.

Robby was a bit on the simple side, but he could work the cash register like a charm. As long as everything had a price written on it, he didn't have any problem with tapping the numbers into the cash register and getting it to open. He'd count out the change, slow and thorough, and hand the customer a receipt with a big smile on his face.

I found out Robby was honest, too. When he saw that twenty-dollar bill on the floor, he gave it to me instead of putting it in his pocket. So I trusted him with running the front of the store and stayed in the back trying to figure out what was what.

Soon enough I got the hang of ordering, marking, and counting all the stuff that came in and went out of the store. It's what they call stock inventory. I didn't know a wrench from a screwdriver, but Robby did, so we got along fine. I even hired old Mr. Herman to look after the books, so I didn't have to bother with math or anything like that.

I was living in a nice house, running a nice business, and bored out of my mind. I didn't have any friends and didn't know how to make any, not being single, not being married, too young for widowhood, too old for burping, and no babies hanging on, so their mothers and me could make friends. I worked the store in the daytime and watched television at night until I thought my eyes would fall out.

That's when I met Geoffrey McPherson. He breezed into the outskirts of town and set up shop as an artist. He painted, did sculptures and pottery, and welded strange looking things out of metal parts he found in the local junkyard.

Then he'd set them out in front of his studio right off old Route 56 and wait for somebody to drive by and buy them. Nobody did.

When he came into the hardware store looking for a deal on nuts and bolts, I knew then and there he was for me. He wasn't as old as Wayne had been, something like his early thirties, and he had those smoldering brown Cary Grant eyes I saw in *An Affair To Remember*. I was done for.

Three weeks later, we were married, and on our wedding night, I climbed on top of him and said, "Now, Geoffrey, I'm going to show you what a husband and wife do, so don't be fearful."

He laughed, and for one whole week showed me loving like I didn't know existed until I signed those papers. Then he beat me within an inch of my life, threw me out of Wayne's house, and took over the hardware store.

I hid out at Grandma's house, not talking to anybody. Her house was the one thing Geoffrey didn't take from me 'cause it was on the other side of town, rundown, and practically worthless.

Days later, Robby showed up ringing the doorbell and banging on the door. When I finally opened it, Robby stood there, breathing hard, and staring daggers at me.

"Why didn't you tell nobody where you was?" In one hand, Robby carried a small, brown paper bag, in the other some daisies. He handed me the flowers. "These here are from my yard. The ones Pearl didn't eat. She ain't much of a hound to look at, but she's otherwise a good dog. I thought you'd like them, Miss Corliss."

I opened the door wide and stood back. "Come on in, Robby, but don't call me Miss Corliss any more. I'm not your boss now. Corliss will do."

"Yes, ma'am," he said, stepping inside.

I shut the front door, headed for the kitchen, and plopped the daisies into the glass of water I'd been drinking at the sink when the doorbell rang. I don't know how long I'd been just standing there, looking out at the old black walnut tree. I carried the flowers to my grandma's yellow kitchen table and set them in the center.

"They're pretty," I said, sitting down in a ripped green vinyl chair, the one with the rickety legs. I pointed Robby to the sturdier one. He sat, never taking his eyes off me, and shuffled around in the teeny chair as if he had something real important to say.

"Why didn't you tell nobody what he done to you, Miss Corliss? He told me you had the Asiatic flu. And why don't you answer your phone, Miss Corliss? Or doorbell neither? I been calling and calling. I come by two or three times, too, since I found out. Where you been?"

"I guess I've been mostly sitting in the back yard under the walnut tree. You can't hear the phone or doorbell from there. What are you doing here, anyway? You should be at work."

"I was fired this morning."

"Fired! Why?"

"I overheard Mrs. Havershaw talking with her sister over in plumbing supplies. She said she seen the whole thing looking through her kitchen window, him beating you and throwing you out of your own house."

"She always was a busybody, even when Wayne was alive."

"She takes pride in being the first to know everything going on, that's for sure. Anyway, I went to Mr. Geoffrey, and I asked him if he done what she said he done, and he fired me. I didn't even know where you were." He leaned in, studying my face. "You look pretty awful, Miss Corliss, but your eyes will heal up. How are you doing?"

"I did myself in, Robby, but I'm sorry I took you with me. Are you going to be able to get another job now?"

"I'll be all right. Juanita, down at the café, said she'd let me wash dishes for her on Wednesdays and Thursdays."

"Doesn't sound like much money."

"Don't need much. I live in that old trailer my daddy left me."

"Out by the quarry?"

"Yes ma'am, me and Pearl."

"That's good." I got up with a sigh. I sighed a lot these days when I wasn't staring out at that old black walnut tree. "Want some coffee?"

"Sure." He watched me fill the pot and put it on the stove. "He shouldn't have hurt you, Miss Corliss. He shouldn't a done that. Maybe you should fight for what he took."

I shook my head. "I don't have any fight in me." I looked around. "This is what I got now, what my grandma left me."

"Still, it don't seem right, Miss Corliss."

"Maybe not, but Wayne left his house and store to me as his wife, and six months later, I get a new husband and give them over to him. I was about as smart as a toad sitting in the middle of the road."

"You're smart enough when you think about it," Robby said.

"Am I?"

"Sure. Even when I try, I can't be as smart as you. I'm smarter than Pearl, but that's about all."

The coffee was done, and I got up and poured two cups. Robby and I sat together, drinking coffee, him with milk and sugar, mine black, and we didn't talk for over an hour. Finally, I said, "I expect people are laughing at me for marrying him in the first place. The good folks of Ash Flat probably say I asked for it. That's what I say, myself."

"Nobody's laughing at you. They want to be your friend, if you'll just let them." His voice was sincere and sweet, but I didn't want to hear it.

"I have never been a bigger fool, Robby," I said. Then I started to cry.

Robby looked real alarmed and patted my hand. "There, there, Miss Corliss."

I pulled my hand out from under his and felt a burst of anger.

"Don't you see? I signed those papers. The ones that said everything of mine was his. We were lying in bed, and he was nibbling on my ear; and I don't know, Robby, I signed them. Ever since that night, he started treating me like I was dirt on the back porch. I'm just a big fool. I see myself. I know."

"You ain't a fool, Miss Corliss. Leastways, I don't think so."

"Thank you, Robby." I started to cry again. "But like I say, I'm done for. I don't have anybody now."

"You got me, Miss Corliss. I'm your friend."

"That's true." I wiped my eyes, smiled at him, and got up to refill the coffee cups. "You are, and I thank you for that. That's why I'm sorry I cost you your job." I poured more coffee and sighed again. I sat down, feeling like I weighed about three-hundred pounds. It didn't make sense, but there you are.

"I don't think it's right, you letting him take everything, Miss Corliss, no matter what you signed," Robby said, breaking into my thoughts and putting more milk from the carton into his coffee cup. "Especially with him having another wife back in California and all."

"Say what?"

"Yes ma'am. Leastways, that's what the letter says. Right after the part where she says she isn't going to get the divorce now. I remember she signed it, 'Your Loving Wife.'"

"You saw that letter, Robby?"

"Yes ma'am. Got it right here along with all the bills." He patted the small paper bag.

"Show it to me."

Robby opened the bag and took out a small pile of papers, different sizes, laid one on top of the other. He set the pile next to the daisies, looking from me to them and back at me again.

I rifled through the pile, picked out the letter, and read it aloud. "'My dearest Geoff, this is exciting news about the inheritance from your aunt in Ash Flats…' His aunt?" I interrupted myself. "Why that lying bastard. Excuse my language, Robby."

"That's all right, Miss Corliss. I wonder if his aunt lived nearby, if I knew her."

"He don't have an aunt, Robby. He's just pretending. He means Wayne's house and store."

"Oh."

I sat for a moment then read the rest of the letter in silence. When I finished, I looked up at Robby who was watching me with those burning, blue eyes, trying to strip the thoughts right off me like paint remover.

"When did this come to the store?"

"Day before yesterday, so I opened it like the rest of the mail. He ought to pay them bills, Miss Corliss. Harlan, down at the lumber store, needs his money bad, what with his wife being in the hospital and all."

"You mean Geoffrey isn't paying the bills?" I got sidetracked from the letter.

Robby didn't say anything, just shook his head slowly.

"I wonder why not?" I looked at Robby. "Is the store still bringing in good money, Robby? Like it did before I left?"

Robby nodded. "Ain't right, Miss Corliss. People expect to be paid, and ever since he took over, he ain't paid one bill, just throws them in the trash. I tried to tell him right after I asked him about you. I brought the stack of bills to him, her letter on top, and he wouldn't even look at them. Snatched that stack out of my hand and told me again to get out, that he had fired me.

"He did it right in front of Mrs. Havershaw, too. Then he pushed me to the door and threw the stack in my face, all the time yelling for me to never come back. I thought Mrs. Havershaw was going to lay down and die, she was so shocked."

I looked at the letter in my hand. "It says here she's going to wait for him to call her after he sells off the estate. They're going to start a new life together. I'll bet he's been planning this the whole time."

"Where's this estate? I thought what you had was a hardware store and a house."

"That's one of those legal terms, Robby. I saw it on *Perry Mason*, 'The Case of The Vanishing Model.'"

"Oh."

"Why isn't he paying the bills, Robby? Tell me that."

"Don't know. Can't tell you."

"I wish I had some money, Robby. He froze the bank accounts, and all I got is the thirteen dollars I had in my purse when he threw me out. I could go to Little Rock and get me an attorney. Geoffrey's got the only one in town. I need money to get a lawyer to tell me how to get Wayne's store and house back."

We sat for moment thinking.

"You still got that money in the cracker barrel, Miss Corliss. You could take that."

I stared at him across the table. "I forgot all about that money in the cracker barrel, Robby. How'd you know about it, anyway? I thought nobody knew about that."

He looked embarrassed. "Oh, I saw you put money in there a couple of times when you thought no one was looking. I took most of my money and put it there, too. It's better than a bank. Handier, too."

"You've been putting money under the straw in that old cracker barrel, like I did?" Robby nodded. "Why?"

He shrugged. "I don't need much. It's just Pearl and me in that little trailer, so I keep what I need and put the rest under the straw, just like you done. You can have it."

"How much is under there, do you expect?"

He shrugged again. "Don't know. I put three or four hundred in there, but I seen you had a lot more. It tends to add up, as my daddy used to say."

"I think there's enough for me to go to Little Rock and hire a lawyer, Robby."

He stood up, rattling the old yellow table. "Well, then, let's go get it."

"No, no. Sit down, Robby."

Robby sat.

"We can't let Geoffrey know about the money. He'll try to keep it."

"But it ain't his, Miss Corliss."

"It wasn't his store, neither, but he's got it. Maybe he took it from me, maybe I give it to him, but it's his. He'll say the money's his, and we don't have any right to it. That's what he'll say. The thing to do is wait until tonight, when the store is closed. I still got a key and—"

"He changed the locks, ma'am."

"Oh, sweet Jesus."

"We'll have to use my key." Robby took out a shiny, new key from his shirt pocket. "I didn't get a chance to give it back to him when I left, what with trying to pick up all those bills before they blew away."

I took the key from his hand. "I'll go after he closes the store. I don't know why he was open, anyway, it being a holiday. The streets will be deserted with everybody going to the Fourth of July fireworks. I can sneak in then."

"You going to try to carry out that big cracker barrel by yourself, Miss Corliss? I don't think you can lift it."

"I thought I'd take the cash out right then and there, Robby. I'll bring a little overnight bag. I got that turquoise one my grandma left me. It's scratched up, but it'll do the job."

"If you wait until I go home to feed Pearl, I'll go with you, Miss Corliss. I don't like the thought of you being out that late at night by yourself, what with this being July fourth and all. Going to be a lot of fireworks and drinking, too."

"Truth be told, I'd like the company, Robby, Fourth of July or not. We'll go close on nine o'clock. I'll wait for you here."

He got up and stretched. "Yes, ma'am. I'll feed me and Pearl and then come back."

"Want some supper? I was going to have hotdogs, cut up and fried in bacon grease along with beans. I got coleslaw, too. You can have some. We'll go to the store right after *The Price is Right.*"

"That the game where people guess how much something costs?"

"You don't know *The Price is Right*?"

He shook his head.

"Don't you watch television?"

"No electricity out at the trailer. Running water, though. I use kerosene lamps."

"When you get back, we'll see it together. Then we'll go to the store."

I watched Robby get into his battered-up truck and drive away, thinking that next to Lanie Sue, he was the only friend I ever had. He came back about an hour later. We ate, and guessed all the prices wrong on the game show, and left for the store right around nine o'clock.

The streets were deserted, it being a holiday, and everybody down at the fairgrounds. Even the sheriff was there running the 4-H exhibit, so I didn't think we had to worry about his patrol car driving by.

I put the new key in the new lock of the store, and we went inside, the cracker barrel in the open space near the cash register being the first thing we saw. The shelving stocked with all kinds of things sat in rows behind with wide aisles between. Robby started for the backroom to turn on the lights, but I stopped him.

"Just in case someone drives by, let's keep the lights off, Robby," I whispered and turned on the flashlight I brought instead. "We'll fill this suitcase in the dark and take it back to the house. Oowee, what's that smell? Kerosene? You spilled some kerosene on you when you went back to feed Pearl?"

"No, ma'am," he whispered back. "You would have smelled it before, Miss Corliss." He sniffed the air. "Anyways, it's coming from in the back."

"Well, let's get the cracker barrel emptied out and get out of here. It's spooky in the dark." My flashlight began to dim, and I shook it. The light faded even more. "Oh, sweet Jesus, the battery's going in this thing. Where are the flashlights around here? I forgot where we keep them." I don't know why, but I kept right on whispering. So did Robby.

"Aisle five, Miss Corliss. Watch that shaky shelf off aisle six right before it. I think you got wood rot. I went up and looked at it while you was gone and told Mr. Geoffrey, but he don't pay attention to what I say. It's going to topple over on someone one of these days."

"I'll be careful. Meanwhile, you use this." I handed him the light. "Take the straw out of that barrel and start putting the cash in the overnight bag."

I tiptoed over to aisle five and was groping in the dark for one of those long handled, heavy duty flashlights we sell, when the lights came on in a blaze. I heard the sound of clomping feet running down the middle of aisle six on the other side of me.

Then I heard Geoffrey's voice. "Freeze, boy," he snarled, sounding a lot like the Doberman Pincher out at Harlan's lumberyard.

I straightened up, not daring to breathe, and listened.

"Well, look at this," he said. "Looks like you were robbing the place, Robby boy."

"No, sir," Robby stuttered, "I was just taking what was mine. This money's mine and Miss—"

"It looks like a robbery to me," Geoffrey interrupted.

I crept closer and tried to see what was going on.

"It looks like I'll have to shoot you," Geoffrey said. "A man can't have his store robbed, even if he was planning to burn it down." He began a laugh that ended with that snarl again.

I didn't like this talk about shooting. I came around the back way into aisle six. Geoffrey was standing with his back to me, waving a mean-looking shotgun, aimed at Robby. Robby looked terrified, holding both hands in the air, dollar bills fluttering every which way.

I heard the gun cock right before I put down that new flash light and picked up a nearby shovel on sale for fourteen ninety-nine. I let Geoffrey have it across the back of his head, just like it was a ball and I was hitting a home run. I was always good at softball.

The shotgun went flying out of his hands but mercifully didn't go off. Geoffrey bounced off aisle seven, the one holding screws, nails, nuts and bolts of all shapes and sizes, and then he fell to the floor. Some boxes of stuff came down and landed on top of him. Both Robby and I stared at Geoffrey laying there like a stone.

"He was going to shoot me, Miss Corliss," Robby finally said. "He really was."

"I know." I leaned the shovel back where I took it from. "You can put your hands down now, Robby."

"Yes ma'am." Robby did and moved closer to Geoffrey's body, studying it. Tears spilled onto my friend's cheeks. I went over and took him by the hands, trying to turn him away from what he was looking at.

"Robby. Look at me." I tugged on his hands. "Robby. Pay attention to me, Robby." He forced his eyes back to my face. "It couldn't be helped. He was going to shoot you. I had to do it."

Robby nodded then turned back to Geoffrey's body. "I think he's dead. Look at his eyes. All glazed over. I seen a buck that looked just like him after a hunter got him right through the heart. He wasn't covered with no nails or screws, though."

"Robby, go to the back of the store and turn off the lights again. There's no cause to let anybody who might be driving by know what's going on."

He nodded and ran to the back of the store. I grabbed a paint bucket and threw up in it. Greasy hotdogs don't sit well with what I was doing.

A few seconds later it went black as night. I could hear Robby feeling his way back down the center aisle toward the front of the store. I picked up the new flashlight I took from the bin and lit the way for him.

"Thanks, Miss Corliss. Sure is dark in here, and the smell's real bad in the back. I think Mr. Geoffrey spilled something, I really do."

"Take this." I pushed the flashlight into his hand. "For what I got to do, my old one's good enough. Go back up to the front and get the money from the cracker barrel," I said.

"Whatever you say, Miss Corliss," he said and off he went. "Watch that wobbly shelf, though. I just bumped into it, and it's worse than I thought."

"I'll be careful." I made my way over to the stepladder section, got me one and took it back to aisle six. Then I stood on it and gave that wobbly shelving a couple of hard shoves with all my might close to the top.

Sure enough, it teetered over and landed on top of Geoffrey spilling lead weights, twine, rope, camping equipment, dust, and I don't know what all on top of him.

"Oh, my Lord, Miss Corliss," Robby's shocked voice came from the front of the store. "It come down just like I said it would. You all right?"

"I'm fine, Robby," I said, stepping down from the ladder. "You nearly done?"

"Yes ma'am. That smell of kerosene is stronger now. You smell it?"

"I do," I said, going behind the counter. "Robby, you go wait in the truck with Grandma's overnight bag. I got one last thing to do." I picked up one of the boxes of matches we give good customers with "Wayne's Hardware" written in orange across the top.

Robby waited in the truck while I lit a match and threw it into the kerosene Geoffrey had poured all over the stock in the back room. When the fire took off, I left the stockroom and went out the front door. Robby and I sat in the truck for about fifteen minutes. We watched the fireworks in the distance until the fire in the store began to light up the black night. Then we drove off. Robby took me back to Grandma's, and he went home to Pearl.

I was sitting in the living room watching *Casablanca* on Grandma's old black and white TV when there was a knock at the door. It must have been close to five a.m. I looked out the peephole, and there stood Sheriff Rayhill.

He came from Memphis twenty-seven years ago after he married Oana, Home Coming Queen of nineteen thirty-two. She's one of the Kelpelmeyers that own the feed store. He's been sheriff for as long as I can remember. Nice man. He gave me a ride once when I was ten years old and got caught in a thunderstorm.

"I got some bad news for you, Corliss," he said to me, his bulk filling up the whole doorway.

"Then you'd better come in, Sheriff Rayhill."

He did. "You heard the fire engines?"

I nodded. "Last night, around ten-thirty or eleven. Wayne used to be a part of that volunteer fire department."

"I remember."

"Where were they heading?"

"To your hardware store, Corliss. It burned down."

"No," I said, putting on my best acting job of looking shocked. "What do you mean, it burned down?" I sat down, trying to look innocent. I put my back to the sheriff, but he walked around and faced me.

"It did, Corliss, and it looks like the fire was deliberately set."

Now I was genuinely shocked. "You mean you could tell that right off?"

"Oh, yes. When you've been around a few fires, read a few books on it, you can tell that. Especially when it's as obvious as this one was. Somebody poured what we call an incendiary fluid in the back storeroom. Gasoline, kerosene, something like that."

"How much of it's gone?" I said.

"Pretty much all of it, Corliss, but there's more to tell, and I want you to prepare yourself." He took a deep breath, and I knew what was coming but didn't let on.

"Corliss," he said, sitting down beside me on the couch. "We found your husband's body in the fire. He's gone and I'm sorry."

I wondered if I should grab my face with my hands, act like I loved Geoffrey. I don't have much of the Ingrid Bergman in me, but I knew I had to look surprised, so I tried working on that.

"Oh, my God," I said and turned away from him again. He put a tender hand on my shoulder and patted it.

"There, there," he said. "We think he started the fire for the insurance. According to Leroy Parker, he took out a new policy only last week."

"He did?" I turned and looked at him. "Mr. Parker from the insurance company?"

"That's right, and he's a volunteer fireman. When he saw what was what, he came and told me about the policy. From what we can tell, your husband set the fire in the back of the store and when he was running out, something happened. We don't know quite yet what that was, but it looks like some of the shelves fell on him and knocked him out. If it's any consolation to you, Corliss, he probably didn't feel a thing."

"Oh, it is, Sheriff, it is." I stood, sniffing into the sleeve of my robe. "I'm glad he didn't feel anything."

"I know what a shock this is for you."

I nodded, looking down at my feet.

"And I know things weren't going well between you and your husband."

I shook my head, still looking down at my feet.

"I wish you'd come to me, Corliss. That's what I'm here for. I had to find out on the street about how he beat you up and threw you out."

I shrugged, embarrassed like.

"I could have arrested him," Sheriff Rayhill went on. "I could have put him in jail. All you had to do was come to me, sign a complaint."

I looked up at him, astonished. "I never thought about that."

"I even dropped by here a couple of days ago, hoping you'd answer the door, to see if you wanted to make a formal complaint."

It seemed like everybody I knew in town had been ringing the doorbell while I was sitting in the backyard. "I guess it's too late now for that."

"Someone's going to have to identify the body, Corliss, officially. There's enough of him left to identity."

"Oh, sweet Jesus, do I have to?"

He hesitated. "No, of course you don't. I can have someone else do it and sign an affidavit. I'll get Leroy Parker." He stood up and looked down at me. "Are you going to be all right, Corliss? Should I send Oana over to be with you for a while? I'm sure she's willing."

"No, I'll be all right. When the sun comes up, I'll go out and sit under the black walnut tree. I like to watch the squirrels."

"You don't take Wild Turkey with you, do you? I'd hate to see you start in on that."

I shook my head. "No, sir, I can't stand the stuff. I don't smoke, I don't drink, and I don't do drugs."

"You always were a good girl, Corliss." He patted me on the shoulder again. "Well, I have to go." He headed for the door and turned around. "There's one more thing, Corliss, something you don't want to think about now, but you'll have to face it sooner or later."

I froze.

"Your husband may have done it for the insurance, but according to Leroy, the policy doesn't pay for arson. He burned the store down for nothing. I'm sorry, but you needed to know."

He turned back to the door, hesitated, and went out. I sat back down and watched a rerun of *The Naked City*, *Casablanca* being over, and thought about Wayne's store.

* * * *

Four days later, we held Geoffrey's funeral. The whole town came, paying their respects and wishing me well. Robby showed up wearing a tie, with Juanita's daughter, Jonnette, on his arm.

She's a nice girl, a year or two older than Robby but along the same simple lines and just as sweet natured. I wore black, even though I didn't feel good about it, like I did for Wayne. This was different. I didn't have any feelings for Geoffrey, other than being glad he was gone.

I waited until Jonnette went off looking for some punch and whispered to Robby,

"Remember, what happened that night is our secret. I would appreciate it if you didn't tell anyone, not even Jonnette."

He looked at me with those burning blue eyes and whispered back. "Miss Corliss, what happened that night goes with me to my grave. I give you my word and that's that."

"Yes, it is, Robby, and I thank you."

The sheriff came in looking happy. After giving his condolences again and inquiring after my health, he told me he had some good news and took me aside to tell it.

Geoffrey had taken out a life insurance policy years ago when he'd joined the Army. It was for fifty thousand dollars, payable to any future spouse, which was me. It was enough, the sheriff said, to rebuild the store, if I wanted to. I did and said so. I could see the news spreading around the room just like the fire spread in that storeroom. Good and bad news travels fast in Ash Flats.

* * * *

It wasn't more than a few days later, and I'd moved back into Wayne's house. Sheriff Rayhill showed up again, standing on the porch, and knocking on the screen door. This time he didn't look so happy.

"What is it, Sheriff?" I said staring at him through the screen.

"I have some bad news, Corliss, so I'm glad you come to the door."

"Then you'd better come in." I opened the screen door, and we went inside to the living room and sat down together on Wayne's orange tufted sofa. The sheriff took one of my hands in his, father-like, and patted it.

"Corliss, I want you to be brave, now."

I was being arrested. I knew it. But I tried to be brave.

"Geoffrey McPherson had another wife, one before you, in California."

I had put that woman out of my mind, and now that I knew that's all he meant, I nearly slid off the sofa in relief.

"They were married in Los Angeles ten years ago," he said, "and there's no evidence of a divorce. In fact, we found a one-way train ticket he'd bought for her bound for Ash Flats."

"You mean…"

"That's right, Corliss, the man was a bigamist."

That wasn't what I was going to say. I was going to say something about the lying bastard bringing that woman to my hometown. But I let it pass.

"Corliss," Sheriff Rayhill went on, "you were never legally married to Geoffrey McPherson. He was married to this other woman. She says she was planning on joining him here in Ash Flats come fall. By law, she's the one entitled to his life insurance premium."

"You mean…"

"That right. The money doesn't come to you."

That wasn't what I was going to say. I was going to say something about that bitch woman coming here after what Geoffrey did to me, even if she didn't know about it. But I let that one pass, too.

What I did say was, "I guess this means Wayne's store got burned down, but now it won't get rebuilt."

"Well, that's something I want to talk to you about. Before I came to see you, I did some talking with the town elders. You're one of us, Corliss, and all alone in a misfortune not brought about by your own doing.

"What could happen, if you want, is that Mr. Wilbur at the bank says he'll give you an interest-free, ten-year loan, using this house as collateral. Harlan at the lumberyard says he'll sell you lumber at cost. All you need."

"Even with those bills he has for his sick wife?"

"Even so. And I know a lot of carpenters who will work for less money than they normally do to help you out, my son being one of them. What do you say, Corliss? Are you going to let this town help you get back on your feet?"

"I don't know what to say. I…" I broke off.

"You're going through a rough patch. It's the least we can do."

I stared at him hard for a moment. "He was going to shoot Robby."

He returned my hard stare. "Whatever happened before today, Corliss, is in the past. It's the future we're concentrating on now."

"But what if you did something in the past you regret?"

"We all have, but it's come and gone. That's why it's called the past."

"You mean anything that happened before…is…in the past?"

"That's what I said."

"It don't matter that—"

"Corliss," he interrupted. "Clean out your ears. It's the past. It's over. The man who deceived you, beat you, and dishonored you is dead and buried. It's time for you to move on."

"All right."

* * * *

It's been five years since Wayne's Hardware got rebuilt. Robby, Jonnette and me, we run it together. The loan'll be paid off in another year or two, faster than I thought I could do it. I gave Robby and Jonnette Grandma's house as a wedding present and am glad of it. Robby and Jonnette have been fixing up the place little by little, and I don't say it's a showpiece, but I think Grandma would be proud.

Before Pearl was neutered, she had three pups, Ruby, Sapphire, and Buddy. Sapphire and Buddy live at Grandma's house, too, along with Pearl. I took Ruby. Sometimes I stop by, and we all sit out in the backyard and watch the squirrels. Sometimes I think I can hear Grandma laughing, although it's probably the wind rustling through the leaves of that old black walnut tree.

I named my daughter Miriam after Grandma. I guess you could say I didn't come out as empty-handed from my experience with Geoffrey as everybody first thought. Miriam's four-and-a-half going on thirty, as her Uncle Robby likes to say, and she's smart as a whip.

She's the darling of Ash Flats—that's the truth—and I love her with all my heart. She was worth everything I went through to get her.

Someday I'll leave her Wayne's house and hardware store. I know Wayne would like that. He was a good man. He lived in a good town and so do I, along with my daughter, my friends, and my dog. And now when I hear the doorbell ring, I answer it first thing. Even when it's Mrs. Havershaw from next door.

Dental Plan
Flash Fiction
by
Heather Haven

Dental Plan

Wallace Pitkin had not seen a dentist in 43 years. It was not just that he was a firm believer in *if it ain't broke don't fix it*, but as a child, his father had experienced a horrifying incident. A sloppy dentist and a wayward Novocain-filled needle had left one side of Pitkin Senior's face paralyzed for life.

It was then a family tradition was born. All the Pitkins learned to deal with tooth pain in the same way: aspirin, Tylenol or ibuprophen, washed down with significant shots of whiskey.

During Mr. Pitkin's end-of-the-year physical the doctor noticed the swollen left jaw coupled with the standard Pitkin foul breath.

"You know, Wallace," The doctor said, looking into Mr. Pitkin's hazel eyes, "the health of your teeth affects the health of your entire body. I've been telling you for years to see a dentist. Now I can't okay you going back to the loading dock until you have them taken care of."

"But I only got one more year and I can retire with full benefits," Mr. Pitkin replied.

"It's the best Christmas present you can give yourself. Don't come back to me until you get your teeth fixed."

For three eight-hour days Mr. Pitkin had his mouth worked on by a dentist who sweated profusely and cursed under his breath. Mr. Pitkin refused to have Novocain but the laughing gas had done him just fine. Even the crabby and corpulent Mrs. Pitkin, with whom he hadn't shared a kiss for 15 years, looked pretty good to him at the end of day two.

On day three, Mr. Pitkin was leaving the Gardner, Zucker and Langusto Dental Compound when he realized he was enveloped by the faint sounds of music interspersed with occasional chatter. It was with him wherever he went. If he opened his mouth it got louder. If he closed his mouth and put his hand over his jaw, the volume decreased. This was good for when he was trapped in an elevator or in line at the grocery store. Mr. Pitkin liked the music. It soothed him.

Feeling very mellow, he returned home and his wife met him at the door. Mr. Pitkin grinned at her broadly. His mouth played "Grandma Got Run Over By A Reindeer."

"What the hell is that?" she demanded.

"It's my new fillings. They're picking up this 24-hour a day radio station."

"Well, turn it off. I can't stand Christmas music."

"I can't turn it off. Besides, I like it. Get over yourself, fatso."

Mrs. Pitkin hauled off and hit him across the face as hard as she could.

He slapped her back.

She picked up a nearby frying pan, swung, but missed him by several inches.

One thing led to another.

Céline Dion warbled "O Holy Night," while Wallace Pitkin strangled his wife.

The lawsuit of Pitkin vs. Gardner, Zucker and Langusto is still pending. But the melody lingers on.

Trade-in
Flash Fiction
by
Heather Haven

Trade-In

"Listen, old man, I'm not going to trade you the truck for the horse, and that's final," Samuel said. The short fair-haired owner of the car dealership stood by the hood of a newish pickup. He pulled the zipper of his blue parka up and down in fast, nervous movements, but his eyes were firm.

Rheumy eyes stared back, half hidden by the brim of the low-riding cowboy hat. The tall, gaunt cowboy leaned down, a lit cigarette clenched between his teeth, dark wool peeking out from under his rawhide jacket. He jabbed a twisted finger in the direction of a large, chestnut stallion tied to a lamppost.

"That saddle alone is worth six thousand dollars. There's hand hammered silver on that."

"You can't have the truck," Samuel repeated. This was getting ridiculous.

"Don't make me shoot ya, boy," the old man growled. He opened the door of the truck and jumped inside. "I gotta get to Casper." He searched for keys over the sun visor, found them, started the motor, and sped away.

The younger man watched, then shouted to his employee, who'd been standing nearby, "Ned, phone the police. Then call the pound to come and take this animal away."

Ned ran a coarse hand through gray-blonde hair and ambled over to the horse. "No need for any of that, Samuel. I'll call your mother. She'll send the trailer for Thunder." He patted the horse's rump.

"I don't care if this is Wyoming." Samuel spat. "Dad can't threaten to shoot me if I don't give him what he wants." He strode toward the small, wind-burned building that sat amidst rows of used cars and trucks.

Ned fell in step. "He figures 'cause he gave you this place, he can take from it what he wants."

"Well, he can't. I come home to run the business and he pulls this crap." He slammed the office door shut and shivered. "God, it's cold out there."

Ned poured himself a cup of coffee. Samuel sat down heavily behind his desk.

"He and I, we don't talk, you know. Maybe we never did. I'm not sure why."

"Maybe it just seems like it. You've been gone eight years: college, then the army. You've done a lot of growing up in that time. You left a boy, you come back a man."

They sat for a moment in silence. Samuel turned to Ned.

"I don't think that's it."

"Other things, maybe. My brother is a complicated man."

"What's in Casper, anyway?"

"A horse."

"What does he need another horse for? Something's going on and nobody will tell. Not mom, not dad, not even you. And I always felt like you and me were closer than anybody, Uncle Ned. To tell you the truth, I don't think dad likes me much."

"Some men don't know how to express their feelings, especially ones they think of as weak. He's always loved you, in his way."

"There's a glowing tribute." He let out a big sigh. "I should just leave. Go back to the East Coast."

Ned hesitated then made a decision. "Your dad's sick, Samuel. The big "C." He turned away. "Ironic, isn't it? Our own Marlboro Man with lung cancer. The doctors don't give him more than six-months."

Samuel sat for a time, opened the bottom drawer of his desk, and pulled out a bottle of scotch. Ned put his hand on his nephew's shoulder.

"Six-months can be a lifetime if you play it right. Maybe it's time you two make amends. Could be that's why he brought you back."

"Damn. I should have traded him the truck."

Socks
A Short Story
by
Heather Haven

Socks

Mr. Lipchitz stood in front of his sock drawer with utter contempt. Somehow in the past three days, it had become completely disorganized and that would not do. No, that simply would not do.

The exacting man believed there should be a place for everything and everything should be in its place. His four bedroom, two bath Victorian house with working fireplace was as neat as a pin at all times.

Correction. He had been assured it was a working fireplace when he purchased the foreclosure but, of course, wood fires are extremely un-neat. Electric heat is cleaner. So even though the recently vanished Mrs. Lipchitz preferred a working fireplace, it had never been used.

He slammed the sock drawer closed in a flash of anger. There resulted a bang of wood against wood. The display of emotion surprised him.

He didn't usually show his displeasure except to Mrs. Lipchitz. Going out for groceries, indeed. His sainted mother had been right; deny his wife money and she'd be gone.

He ran a bony finger over the surface checking the drawer and surrounding polished wood for damage. His mother's cherry wood gentleman's dresser, with its elegant silver and onyx inlay, gleamed back at him, unharmed. The gaunt man took a step back, and once again admired the lines of the art deco piece coveted by many a private collector.

"My apologies, my friend, for losing my temper," he said with a slight bow. "It certainly isn't anything you've done and won't happen again."

Glancing at his wristwatch, he crossed the room appreciating the thick, Persian carpet beneath his feet. He relished the memory of how he'd garnered it for a ridiculously low price at auction several years before. Then he headed down his eighteenth century, carved mahogany staircase towards the living room.

Being a Certified Public Accountant may have been his livelihood, but his life's work was attaining treasures at discounted prices. He made it his business to find out who was in desperate need of money, declaring bankruptcy, going out of business, or had "passed over," as his own sainted mother had done five years before.

Of course, it did help that his mother had left him quite a legacy upon her passing, a point of which the not currently present Mrs. Lipchitz had reminded him countless times. Through the years, he had obtained many fine pieces and his home reflected his exquisite taste and acquisitional habits. The contents of his home became not only his possessions, but steadfast friends.

Mr. Lipchitz stepped into the living room and surveyed it with immense satisfaction. His eyes beheld the sparkling amethyst and lead crystal chandelier, fine paintings, porcelain figurines, museum quality furniture, and rare Oriental rugs, all obtained for a fraction of their value by his cunning negotiating and bidding skills.

Show me a person in a perilous position, he would say, and I will show you an anxious seller. Therefore, wherever there was a venue for the luckless or needy, Mr. Lipchitz would be there, checkbook in hand.

He stopped before the marble mantel of his fireplace and looked again at his platinum watch, another fabulous buy from a suicidal stockbroker. It was nearly quarter to the hour. Focusing his attention upon the antique Swiss clock, he grasped his restless hands behind his back and waited.

He had procured this fine example of an antique cuckoo clock eight-months previous. Over two hundred years old, it contained three sets of elaborate, moving figures, each announcing the hour, half-hour or quarter-hour, accompanied by intricate, musical chimes.

It was the quarter-hour which worried him. A yellow-haired maiden would appear carrying two milk buckets, a bluebird resting on one of them. As the girl glided in her arc across the façade of the clock from left to right, a small, brown dog followed her. The dog was supposed to wag its tail in its passage but, so far had not. That was unacceptable.

Since purchasing the clock, Mr. Lipchitz labored over it in his basement workshop every evening from seven forty-five until nine-thirty p.m. exactly. With the aid of manuals, obscure springs, complex parts and lengthy conversations with experts, Mr. Lipchitz felt he had finally achieved his goal. After reconnecting all working parts the previous evening, now was the supreme test. Would the dog repeat his performance on the mantle piece, thereby promising a twice-hourly repetition for many years to come?

Mr. Lipchitz waited anxiously as the clock began to chime. The small door on the left side opened and the milkmaid began her journey from one side to the other. Soon a small, brown dog followed her, wagging its tail. Mr. Lipchitz was elated.

"You're a good boy," he said to the dog. "A good boy."

With a sense of accomplishment, Mr. Lipchitz sat down at his heirloom grand piano, opened the lid, stretched his fingers and prepared to play as he did every evening before dinner. He would begin again the second movement of Mozart's Piano Concerto No. 6 in B flat, and it would be only that piece until it was perfected.

His fingers hovered over the keys then came to rest in his lap. Mr. Lipchitz pursed his lips. An errant thought came into his mind jarring this perfect moment.

What was going on inside his sock drawer? He reflected on the procedure. Each sock was clipped together with its mate before putting them into the hamper. They were washed in the machine and still clipped, placed into the dryer. After they were dried, only then were they unclipped, folded neatly and placed, according to color, into the sock drawer of his fine, gentleman's dresser.

In the unlikely event there appeared a matchless sock, the sock was carefully placed to the left side of the sock drawer until the recalcitrant mate reappeared. That happened only once, when he had foolishly allowed the now missing Mrs. Lipchitz to do his laundry. It never happened when he did the laundry himself, until lately.

For the past few days, more and more pairs were coming out of the dryer sans clips and sans mates. The left side of the drawer was becoming filled with mateless socks. Just how many, he wondered? Discarding his normal routine, he rose to return to his bedroom to find out.

He went to his walk-in closet, picked up one of the two empty wooden laundry baskets kept there for such an occasion, and returned to the gentleman's dresser. Opening it, Mr. Lipchitz removed all the socks and placed them inside the basket.

With a sense of distaste, he carried the basket down the stairs, into the kitchen, and emptied it onto the original nineteen-twenty's, white porcelain table that had once lived in the kitchen of Hearst Castle. He separated the mateless socks into pairs and colors then bit his lower lip to keep from crying out.

One blue, two odd black, and four various shades of brown mateless wonders stared up at him as he stared down at them. He counted no less than seven missing socks before slipping a nitroglycerin tablet between yellowing teeth to quell an erratic heart.

"This will not do," Mr. Lipchitz said aloud. He gathered up the socks and strode into the laundry room. He stood in the square, white room, complete with a low, stone hewn garden sink. Across from the sink sat the washing and drying machines, acquired from the sale of an M.I.A. soldier's possessions.

He studied the washer, clean, white and new.

"No, you are all right," he decided, patting the top loading washer several times on the lid. "Everything is all right going in and coming out of you."

He turned to the dryer. It also sparkled clean, new, and white.

"But you! I believe you to be the troublemaker. What have you done with my socks?"

He kicked the dryer squarely in the center of the door. Waving the offending socks in the air, he hurled them down on top of the appliance. His deceased mother's pique café curtains quivered in the window from the slight movement of air.

The man repeated the question. "Well? What have you done with my socks?"

"I ate them," a deep bass voice replied, resonating within the small room.

Shocked, Mr. Lipchitz backed up and, in doing so, tripped over his own foot and fell into the Tuscan garden sink containing seedlings ready to be planted in his pristine and well-organized garden.

"Who said that?" he asked. Wiping dirt and small leaves from the back of his slacks, he looked around for the source. "Who said that?"

"I did, you prissy butthole. You asked me what I did with them and I told you. Now go away."

The voice seemed to come from the dryer. Mr. Lipchitz stared at it, his eyes wide with fear.

"What…what did you say?" He clutched at the sink behind him.

"I said go away, you sniveling snot rag! What are you, deaf, as well as ugly?" The masculine voice took on more of a grating tone with each word it spoke. "Get lost! Take a hike! Or give me more socks. Is that clear enough for you?"

Mr. Lipchitz fought to remain calm, his mind racing. This could not be an intruder. He would have heard the alarm go off; he tested it every day. The doors and windows of his home were locked, always. The security system was sophisticated and on, as it was every single moment of every single twenty-four hours in a day, unless he was in the garden or garage, where he had not been for several days. He had been toiling downstairs in his shop on the dog's tail.

"How can this be happening? What's going on?" He said as he looked all around him.

"Heh, heh, heh," chortled the dryer. "Gotcha, didn't I?"

"All right. All right. That's enough," Mr. Lipchitz replied with a bravado he was not feeling. "This joke has gone on long enough. Whoever you are, come out from behind the clothes dryer. This is not funny."

"Look, you moronic imbecile, you pathetic excuse for a man, do you think anybody could be standing behind me mouthing off and not be seen?"

Even though less than a six-inch space existed between the wall and the dryer, Mr. Lipchitz, nonetheless, craned his neck around to the side of the dryer to see if someone was hiding. No one was there.

"I don't understand," he stuttered.

"You're such a frigging dickhead," the dryer said and began to laugh raucously.

"Stop using language like that," Mr. Lipchitz reprimanded. "This is my house and I won't stand for it."

"Oh, you won't, won't you? If you don't like my language, leave the room. But before you do, throw me a sock. I'm hungry."

"Shut up! How dare you talk to me like that? You're just a dryer."

"Up yours!" the machine drawled. "Got any more blue ones? Those are my favorite. Must be something about the dye." The dryer made a smacking sound. "Yummy!"

"Why, you miserable piece of tin…" Mr. Lipchitz shouted. He bent over and opened the dryer door, looking inside for a hidden child or midget.

"Want to climb in and take a ride, butt-face? It'll cost you one pair of socks and maybe your jockey shorts."

Mr. Lipchitz kicked at the sides of the dryer, scuffing his Bally Oxfords. Then he grabbed both sides of the dryer and began to shake it wildly.

"Shut up, shut up, shut up," he cried again and again. The room echoed with his voice, raspy intakes of breath, and the sounds of clanking metal mixed with strident laughter. His mother's curtains quivered again and again.

"Ooooooo! You're scaring me now!" the appliance said, with a chortle. "What are you going to do, you wuss? You haven't got what it takes to pull me off my foundation. I'm bolted on. Face it, you jackass. Give up and throw me more socks!"

A scream of rage erupted from the depths of Mr. Lipchitz' very being. He took hold of the back of the dial plate with one hand, the dryer opening with the other and began rocking back and forth with all his might. The more he pulled and pushed, the more the dryer taunted him. His face turned red and sweat poured from his body. His muscles strained, ached, and then trembled. Finally, the bolts that secured the dryer to its frame began to rip loose with a shrill, tearing sound.

But Mr. Lipchitz was beyond hearing that. He was too busy feeling the searing, hot pain in his chest right before he pulled the dryer on top of him.

The next morning, the back door was unlocked and a middle-aged woman peeked inside. She stepped over the threshold, turned off the warning pings of the alarm system, and tiptoed across the room to the stiff hand protruding from beneath the dryer.

She ascertained that dead was dead and went to the wall behind the dryer. Humming a smart tune, she withdrew a small tool from her bag and unscrewed the cover to the phone jack. Nestled inside were a small microphone, speakers and wires. She placed the electronics in her handbag and returned the cover to the wall.

Tottering on platform heels, the short, squat woman walked through the house to the living room and toward one of the hand blown, bevel-edged, double windows framed magnificently in rose-gold brocade. She pulled back one side of the opulent drapes just enough to signal her young and nubile lover in the waiting car. The lover pulled away and left her to the next task.

Removing a raw onion wrapped in a hanky plus a cell phone from her bag, she sat down in a genuine Queen Anne walnut wing chair, resplendent in the original blue silk velvet. She dialed nine-one-one while dabbing at her eyes with the onion. As she waited for the operator to answer, Mrs. Lipchitz looked around her and thought, "Ka-ching, Ka-ching."

Boo
Flash Fiction
by
Heather Haven

Boo

Cliff adjusted the eye-patch and scrutinized the handsome pirate's reflection in the full length mirror. From black leather boots to golden earring, he looked real enough to sail the seven seas. And just as lusty. Women liked that.

"You're one good looking son of a bitch, Cliffy Boy, if I do say so myself." He let out a raucous laugh. "Especially now that you're a widower."

The doorbell rang. He grumbled about early trick-or-treaters as he went to the door. He wanted to leave momentarily for the Halloween party, hoping to score big with a hot employee from the life insurance company. It was so nice when the company paying off for your wife's demise also put out. Two short months of her being dead and he'd never seen so much action. All those babes just waiting to comfort him.

"Ahoy there, matie!' He flung open the door, posed then looked up and down the hallway. There was no one. Out of the corner of his eye, he saw a small creature scurry across the threshold and into his penthouse apartment.

"Damn it to hell," he bellowed and turned around to see his dead wife's black cat run through the living room and out onto the terrace, the terrace from where he'd helped his wife to her untimely but necessary death. She'd been cramping his style, plus there was all that lovely money.

He would have tossed the beast over the railing, too, if he could have caught it. But right after the 'accident,' it ran out into the hallway meowing at the front door of their nosy neighbor, who'd scooped it up and took it inside. Ever since, anytime he would step into the hallway to go to work or out on a date, the cat would be there, staring at him from the other side of the neighbor's transom.

Now the cat leapt onto the ledge of the terrace railing and turned around. It crouched, tail lashing back and forth, black fur rippling in the wind off the Hudson River. Sharp green eyes glared at Cliff in an accusatory way.

"Damn it to hell," Cliff repeated, following the cat out onto the terrace. He closed the sliding glass door, trapping him and the cat outside. The Manhattan skyline was darkening and the feline's ebony-colored fur blended in with the on-coming night. But its emerald eyes glittered more intensely than any light in the city's panoramic view behind.

"So you want to play, do you? Well, you're dead meat, cat. I'm sick of dealing with you."

The cat growled and hunkered down atop the cement railing separating the terrace from the earth below.

Cliff moved forward, unsheathing the large plastic sword from his belt. "I don't have to come near you," he yelled, raising his arm and preparing to strike. "Just a couple of swipes with this –"

"Now, Cliff," a feminine voice chastised. "That's hardly fair."

"Who said that?" Cliff dropped the play sword and staggered back, banging into the closed glass door. He felt his heart thud in his chest. "Who's out here? Show yourself! Who are you?" But he recognized the voice.

"You know who I am." The tone was melodious yet dripping with venom. "It's one thing for you to do away with me, but an innocent little animal? That's too much, Cliff, even for you."

He looked in the direction of the voice and saw a small shimmering cloud, hardly more than a vapor, forming into the features of a face, his wife's face.

Cliff let out a short yelp, turned and scratched at the handle of the sliding glass door. It slid open and he fell back into the room. He spun around to see the apartment, nothing more. Sounds of his heavy breathing filled the spacious room.

It must have been the curry he had for lunch or the spicy lamb shish kabob! Well, never again, he vowed, with a shaky laugh. Time for that party, he thought, and stepped forward. An icy wind raged on his face, so cold his eyes began to tear.

"Where do you think you're going, Cliff?"

The countenance was now in front of him, drawing closer and more solid, emerald green eyes flashing. Pushed back by the vision, Cliff found himself outside again, panicky steps taking him along the perimeter of the elegant, plant-laden terrace.

He neared the cat still on the handrail. It reached out, swiped at his hand, and drew blood. Thrown off balance, Cliff tripped over one of the potted plants his wife so dearly loved, the ones that seemed to get watered whether he did it or not.

The cat screeched. Talons and fangs struck again. Two sets of flickering green eyes watched as Cliff toppled over the railing.

On the way down forty-two stories to the pavement below, and in between his screams, Cliff thought of something odd. He'd never noticed before how his late wife's eyes and those of the cat looked one and the same.

Dance Steps
A Short Story
by
Heather Haven

Dance Steps

Agapantha Rouenne Collier was born on Bastille Day in Paris, Texas, and never saw the irony. She was the eldest daughter of a flamboyant yet neglectful couple who preferred flowers to children. Her four younger sisters were named Clematis, Daisy, Gladiola, and Peony.

As a child, Agapantha strove to live a provincial life, despite society's changing roles for women. She grew into a plain, no-nonsense woman blessed with a good mind, unending common sense, and a stern but fair disposition. Agapantha married well, and for what she considered to be all the right reasons.

She, in turn, was the ideal wife for portly William Collier, a competent and dependable banker living in the small town. He wanted a bedrock of a wife who would keep a good house, cook a good meal, give him fine children, and make few demands, with never a chance of scandal or worry. For twenty-seven years Agapantha Rouenne Collier was such a wife.

On June 28th, at three thirty-five p.m. to be exact, Agapantha met a purveyor of fine footwear, or shoe salesman, named Julio Rodriguez. He had thick black hair, the very slightest of Puerto Rican accents and danced the tango like an Argentine. That was only to be expected, as he was also a part time dance instructor.

With her children grown and time on her hands, Agapantha took a series of tango lessons from Julio Rodriguez. She was a changed woman.

Julio Rodriguez found Agapantha to be one of the most charming and entertaining women he'd ever met. He loved her wry humor. He admired her deep blue eyes, which sparkled perversely when they talked. He appreciated her slender ankles and shapely legs when they danced the tango.

At thirty-five years of age, he brought out the best in the older woman. At forty-six, Agapantha found her fading youth replenished.

The first to notice were her twin daughters, studying piano at the Music Conservatory in Flower Mound, Texas.

"What's up with Mom?" said Patricia. "It's been five or six weeks since I've seen her. She doesn't come to our concerts, anymore."

"I don't know, but Dad mentioned she told him she was with us last Saturday night. I didn't say anything, but she wasn't." replied Pamela.

"Maybe he got it wrong. You know how he is," said Patricia.

William Collier was not the type of man to pay attention to the comings and goings of his wife or family, busy as he was concentrating on his career. The twins shrugged their shoulders and went about their business, knowing how he was.

Agapantha's son, William Junior, was the second to notice. Several weeks later he called the girls.

"What's up with Mom?" he said from Baltimore, Maryland, where he was attending the Peabody Institute of Music. They were a very musical family even though Agapantha had never, herself, learned to play an instrument, being too busy first as the bedrock of her parent's home and then her own.

"She usually calls every three or four days but I haven't heard from her in weeks," William Junior said.

"Have you called her, William?" asked Patricia.

"I don't have time. Besides, Mom is Mom. She usually phones me."

"Why don't you call her?" said Pamela, on the other line. "We're pretty busy or we would."

He thought about it. "No, it's not necessary. Besides, I've got a lot going on right now. I'm up for first cellist. As long as I know Mom's all right, I'll wait until she calls me."

All three agreed on a plan of action, which was to do nothing. They hung up and went about the collective concerns of their lives.

William Senior was the last to notice. Being vice-president of the local branch of a nationwide bank, with an impending merger looming overhead kept his mind occupied and his conscience oblivious. The merger was only the latest of his job preoccupations.

If he hadn't been searching for his high school yearbook to share with a client, he might not have found the red patent leather stilettos with a small bow on the back of each heel. The shoes were on the top closet shelf, pushed way in the back. He'd never seen anything like them in their closet before.

He shoved aside his father's old service revolver resting in a cardboard box and there they stood, next to silver high-heeled sandals with glittery hearts on the straps. He'd never seen those before, either.

William picked up one of the high-heeled sandals and turned it over, noting the sole was used, but not overly. He replaced the shoes just so, the yearbook, and the cardboard box containing the old service revolver. Deep in thought, William stepped off the stool, and looked around him, as if for the first time.

A slight film of dust covered the usually gleaming furniture. The bed was hastily made. Underneath, several dust bunnies ran amuck. There was a week's worth of dishes in the dishwasher and the small herbal garden over the sink needed watering. William watered the plants.

* * * *

The next day, instead of going to work, William parked his Lincoln Town Car at the corner of the block and waited. Agapantha came out of the house about an hour later and got into her car. William followed. She drove to Bowden's Dress Shop and bought many things, as if she were going on a long trip.

Burdened down with packages, she crossed the street and went into a luggage store. There she purchased a piece of red luggage, the kind you pull behind you, even though they had a full set of sturdy, gray suitcases stored in their basement.

She put everything in the trunk of her car and drove away. William trailed her to a beauty parlor across town and through the glass window, saw them do something to her hair and face.

When Agapantha came out, she looked like a different woman; a woman he didn't know. William further noticed that instead of her sturdy Rockport Walking Shoes, she was wearing the red patent leather stilettos.

Met at the curb by a taxicab, she transferred the recent purchases from the trunk of her car into the cab. She and the cab raced away, leaving her car parked on the street. William followed again.

The Ralston-Nixon Residential Hotel was in the heart of town. Struggling with the luggage and packages, she emerged laughing from the cab. William parked two cars down, where he watched her go inside the hotel. He got out and waited in a nearby coffee shop. It had bad coffee but a good view of the hotel.

Agapantha came out three hours later without the luggage or packages. The straps to her red heels were hanging around her ankles, as if she had hastily put them on. Her recently coifed hair was in disarray. She had a smile on her face.

William watched Agapantha, his stern, plain, no nonsense wife, run fingers through her unkempt hair in an effort to fix it. Another cab showed up. She got in and sped away.

"The woman that just left here dropped this wallet," he said, offering up his own as evidence of the fact to the hotel clerk.

"Mrs. Rodriguez?" said the thin, balding man. "I'm not surprised. Last week she dropped a shopping bag when she was getting on the elevator." He leaned in conspiratorially.

"I took it up to their room. She hadn't even known. Inside was one of those black lace thingies with feathers all around the bottom, you know. I bet it kept her neck warm that night. Gave me a great tip." He winked. "I'll take that for you." He reached out for the wallet but William drew it back.

"That's all right. I know where she's going. I'll give it to her, myself." He left, got into his car, and drove home.

That evening while she answered her emails in the study, William went through Agapantha's handbag and found a hotel room key, number four-thirty-three. He went out later on the pretense of fetching papers at his office. At the Ralston-Nixon Residential Hotel he saw a different front desk clerk, this one with dandruff powdering his black suit. William stopped at the front desk.

"May I help you?" The clerk's voice was soft but nasal.

"Yes, I'd like to see Mr. Rodriguez. He's in room four-thirty-three, I believe?"

"Yes, but Mr. Rodriguez isn't here," the room clerk replied. "He's at the Roseland Ballroom, as he usually is most nights."

Puzzled, William blinked several time before saying, "I see. Thank you."

William went to Roseland. After asking around, he spotted Julio Rodriguez, a man who seemed to him like a gigolo, dancing the tango with an older woman. For over an hour he watched this Julio Rodriguez dance with several older women, most of them the same age as his wife, if not older. Appalled, William went home.

* * * *

The next day, once again not going to work and still in possession of the room key, William set out for the hotel. Instead of stopping at the desk, he went into the elevator as if he was registered, and up to the room number on the key. He unlocked the door aware of his pounding heart. William knew it was wrong, but his rage outweighed any sense of right or wrong. He went inside.

It was easier than he thought. No one seemed to hear or notice until it was too late. Afterward, he drove around in his Town Car for hours, and then went home.

"I've done something terrible," he said to Agapantha, who was sitting in an easy chair, staring out the bedroom window.

"I know." She rose and faced him slowly. "I saw the six o'clock news."

William sat heavily on the edge of their bed. "I don't know what came over me." He looked down, burying his face in his hands. "I don't know what came over me."

Agapantha was silent. He continued to mumble through his fingers.

"I didn't notice the crowd gathering under the window until after I threw all the shoe boxes out. There must have been three dozen pairs of shoes."

"Thirty-four pairs, actually. I counted them."

"Then I threw out all the bags of clothes, including the lingerie. I kept throwing things out the window, one after another. The red suitcase was the last. I fled when I heard the elevator doors open and someone running down the hall towards the room. I just made it down the stairs in time. I don't know what came over me," he repeated again. William finally looked up at her. "Are you really going to leave me for that man?"

She said nothing. William's eyes scrutinized her face.

"I can't believe any of this," he said, his head dropping down again. "I've been wracking my brain, trying to figure out what's happened to us."

Agapantha spoke. "The newsman said the police couldn't tell from the crowd's account who it was throwing the clothes and shoes out the window. They only know the man who rented the room by the month was out of town on business, so it couldn't have been him. They're baffled. I knew it was you. I recognized you from the description, but nobody else knows."

"I don't care about what's on the news or what anybody else knows."

"You don't?" She rose from the chair, her voice carrying emotion for the first time.

He shook his head. "Don't leave me, Aggie. I can't live without you." He reached out his hand.

"It seems to me you hardly notice whether I'm here or not," she said, not taking his hand, but staring down at him.

Shocked, he looked up. "How can you say that?"

"William, when you've been ignored most of your life, you think that's the way it is; the way it has to be. But then someone comes along and you find out you don't have to feel so lonely or unappreciated."

"Have I done that to you, Aggie? Made you feel unappreciated?"

She was quiet but nodded. "Not just you. My parents, my sisters, even my children. It's not that anyone treats me badly. No one's treats me any way at all. I'm just there. It's mostly my own fault, I see that now. Then Julio came along, and I learned it could be different."

"My God," William said, his voice breaking, hand still extended. "Aggie, I can change. I can be better. We have so much. Don't throw it away. Give me a chance. Give him up, Aggie, please. I love you. Give him up."

She said nothing but took his hand.

* * * *

"I'm glad I wasn't there when he arrived," said Julio. "He might have shot me."

"No, that would have gone totally against everything I know of his character. But just in case, I removed the firing pin from his father's revolver. It was prudent to send you out of town, though, once I realized he took the key from my handbag. I'm sorry about your shoe samples. Of course, I'll pay for them."

"Weren't you beginning to think he'd never get it, Ags?" asked Julio. "I was."

"I kept giving him clues until he paid attention. I took a chance he might love me enough to fight for me."

"We took a chance." Julio paused. "But it was worth it, sweetie. You got your husband back. Now Reggie and I can move on and open our dance studio. No more shoes."

"Did you sign the lease?"

"Yes, for three-years, instead of one. I love the steamy nights of Boca Raton. We're going to make this work."

"Good for you." Agapantha reflected. "I never had much of a dream. And it's too late now."

"It's never too late. Look at Reggie and me."

"That's what I admire about you, Julio, the way you look at life. It's inspiring. I made a deposit into your account yesterday."

"Ags! I told you, you didn't have to do that. I didn't do it for the money."

"I know. But money is something I have to spare and it's my way of saying 'thank you.' I couldn't have done this without your help. Besides, ten thousand dollars will be a nice cushion for your new business."

"Well, I'm glad it's over," said Julio. "Reggie was beginning to get jealous, foolish hag." They both giggled.

"If you ever need more cash, you have but to write," Agapantha said.

"You are so good, Girlfriend."

"And this is goodbye. We'll never meet again. I gave William my word."

"You are so bad, Girlfriend."

The Ring
A short Story
by
Heather Haven

The Ring

She found the ring around six in the morning, at the bottom of the forward portside staircase, third floor, outside deck. Lusa often came up to walk the largest deck early in the morning before guests were up and around. This was her opportunity for fresh air and a look at the sea and sky. Once she began her cleaning day, she would only see them fleetingly through portholes.

Lusa's real name was Lyudmila Bostranovich. This was her first job as a steward on a cruise ship. While working on the Galaxy Cruise Lines during one of its weekly runs on the Mexican Rivera, she was about to embark on an unexpected adventure that would change her life forever.

At first Lusa thought the multicolored sparkle was a piece of crumpled foil discarded by one of the guests during the night. She almost left it but her work ethic got the better of her. She reached down and, surprised, picked up a large cocktail ring whose fiery stones glittered wildly in the California sun.

It was an unusual teardrop design, with a centered, six-carat opal surrounded by sixteen perfect half-carat diamonds. Forty-seven smaller sapphires, richly dark as to look almost black, were set so close together they twinkled as one in their platinum setting. Lusa didn't know all of that, of course, but she knew at a glance the ring was valuable.

Hesitating for only a moment, she decided to turn the ring over to Lost and Found on her way to her job. She prayed God would understand her hesitation, caused by her being a struggling woman with a waiting child and husband half a world away, so far from home she couldn't afford to call them more than once a month. Both she and her husband, Igor, worked alternating six-month renewable contracts for different cruise lines. This was mostly due to policies disallowing married couples to work together.

But an alternate work schedule, while not ideal, permitted one of them to be home with their thirteen-year old daughter, Natasha, at all times. Home was Ukraine, an economically desperate country. In four years time they hoped to save enough money to buy a house and send their daughter to university.

* * * *

"I found this ring and I would like to turn it in," she said in a strong, but understandable Slavic accent. The Second Purser, looking crisp in his starched, white uniform, nonetheless yawned in her face, as he came out of his inner office to stand behind the counter.

Mr. Volpi was a young Italian-American who usually shared the late night, twelve-hour shift with another Second Purser, a Miss Gonzales. The gorgeous Miss Gonzales had been ill that evening, so instead of passing the time flirting with her he got to think about how tired he was. Mr. Volpi was cranky and wanted to sleep. He did not want to concentrate on some dreary steward standing in front of him. He did not want to write up a lost and found report, especially minutes before his shift ended.

"Oh, Christ," he griped. "That looks like a cheap piece of costume jewelry to me. Probably one of those trinkets from the Mardi Gras party up on the Lido deck last night. Why don't you just keep it or throw it overboard? What's your name, anyway?"

"Lyudmila Bostranovich, but please to call me Lusa. I am assigned to cleaning the eighth floor cabins, portside, numbers eight-two-two zero through eight-two-five-zero," she repeated by rote.

She continued, "I do not think, Mr. Volpi, this ring is for the costume. It is expensive, I think. A woman is upset at its loss; I do believe what I say is true." She extended the ring forward, forcing him to take it in his hand.

Mr. Volpi let out a martyred sigh and set the ring down on the counter without looking at it. He reached underneath the counter for the necessary forms.

"Oh, all right," he began impatiently. "Where did you find it?" For the first time Mr. Volpi looked directly at her. What he saw was a pretty, gamine woman, looking younger than her thirty-five years. He leaned over the counter and smiled encouragingly at her.

She told him the specifics and was rewarded, not with him filling out forms, but with a stroke of her cheek. Lusa's eyes flashed in anger and she slapped at his hand. The young man backed off, becoming cold and condescending. He looked at the ring and picked it up again.

"You know, Lucy…"

"Lusa," she said.

"Lu-sa," he repeated pointedly. "You know what I'm going to do, Lu-sa?"

"No, I do not. What are you going to do?"

"I am going to throw this piece of crap into the trashcan right over there." He gestured to a large receptacle near the door to his inner office. "And I'm not going to fill out any forms for it, either."

Contemptuously, he tossed the ring into the trashcan without taking his eyes off of Lusa. "Now, why don't you get to your job, wherever that is, Lu-sa, and leave me alone?" Mr. Volpi ripped up the Lost and Found form and went back into the inner office, slamming the door behind him.

Confused but determined, Lusa retrieved the ring from the trashcan and put it in her pocket. She pondered the problem. She could go to her floor supervisor but she had not found it while on duty, so that might be an incorrect move. Early life behind the then iron curtain had taught her once a person of authority rebuffed her, she should not repeat the error by pursuing that path any further. Her father's three-year stint in a soviet prison as a dissident lived with her always.

If Mr. Volpi wasn't going to do something about this, she decided, she would search for the owner herself, although she wasn't sure how to go about it. There were nearly fifteen hundred passengers and eight hundred crewmembers.

Her twelve-hour workday started at eight in the morning and went until eight or nine in the evening, but she had her treasured breaks and meals.

Perhaps she could wander the corridors hoping to find a clue as to the owner. She might hear from one of the other stewards about a distraught woman looking for a missing piece of jewelry. She would keep her ears open.

If not, when they got to port in two days time, she would go to a policeman in Puerto Vallarta on her day off. She hadn't heard much about the Mexican police but they couldn't be any worse than what she'd experienced in the former Soviet Union.

Having recently acquired her visa, Lusa was finally allowed to leave the ship. She decided she would spend her first day on foreign soil in a Mexican police department.

Whoever lost this ring must have it back. She had found it and it was her responsibility to return it to the owner. With a sense of obligation, she went to her station and began her long and tiring day.

* * * *

The Captain's doorbell rang with lunch. It was wheeled in on a serving cart covered by a linen cloth, complete with a red rose in a sterling silver bud vase.

Captain Sven Yurman had just removed the lid and was inhaling the fragrance of the chef's specialty, still bubbling in its juices, when a knock on the door interrupted his reverie.

After inquiring who it was, he flung open the door. "Ah, Jeremiah," he said to the slim, black doctor dressed in a crisp, white uniform. "Come on in and have some Lobster Thermador! There's more than enough for two."

Doctor Jeremiah Grant stepped inside shaking his head. "Sven, Sven, you know what I have said about your cholesterol levels. You should have a salad with no dressing and a piece of skinless chicken or you will not live to see retirement."

"Is that what you came here to do? Ruin my lunch?" the captain asked with humor in a barely discernible Swedish accent. He sat down tucking a cloth napkin under his chin.

"Just smell that lobster!"

The Jamaican physician walked over and stood by the cart looking out onto the Captain's private deck.

"This is going to be a strange trip, my friend," the doctor said darkly, as he tapped his nose. "You smell the food but I smell the passengers."

"That sounds unappealing," Captain Yurman slurred, his mouth full of seafood.

"Last night a woman comes in asking me for a tranquilizer to help her sleep. A small woman, looking like a bird, she is so small. But on her hand is a large ring that was, well, I can only say it was one honker of a ring." Doctor Grant liked to use what he perceived were American colloquialisms.

"So?" the Captain asked, shrugging. "There are a lot of ladies with bad taste wearing gaudy things. That's what a cruise is all about."

"And she was wearing matching earrings and a necklace, also very large," the doctor went on, ignoring his friend's comment. "They looked ridiculous on her. She was nervous and kept twisting and turning this big ring, so much so I was getting nervous just watching her. When I said to her, 'Be careful, ma'am, not to lose that ring. It looks like it might fall off,' she gasps like this."

The doctor demonstrated in a style reminiscent of a melodrama, clutching at his chest and contorting his face.

"Then she leaps up from her chair and ran out like a woman possessed, without even taking the medicine she came in for with her."

"That is strange," remarked the Captain, pausing with his fork in midair.

"Yes. That is how I know it will be a peculiar trip. This happened before we left port and she has yet to return for the prescription."

"Hmmmm," said the Captain. "Do you remember her name?"

"Of course, I do. Miss Parker, Cora Parker. A very ugly, small woman. I've sent two messages to her cabin, but have yet to hear from her."

The Captain of the Galaxy Star put down his fork, no longer hungry. "Do you think it means anything? I need to retire with full honors. You know that, Jeremiah, in six month's time. I need a spotless record."

"Well, it's already too late for that. Remember the attempted high jacking last year near Bermuda?"

"The Company ruled that wasn't my fault."

"Then there was the food poisoning in the Panama Canal two years before. Six hundred and thirty passengers and crew down. They were suspicious about that one. Did the Company ever find out it was because your friend, the pastry chef, left the refrigerator doors open too long when he was selling off his cakes in port to the locals?"

The Captain's normal ruddy complexion drained of color. "They never proved that and I fired him afterward. Oh, God, Jeremiah, do you think anything is going to happen on this trip? I can't afford anything else. Not if I want full honors and the pension that goes with it."

"I don't know, Sven. We must be vigilant, that's all," he said, sitting down across from his now uneasy friend. "That lobster does look good. Maybe I will have a bite."

* * * *

It was 8:00 pm or twenty hundred hours, nautical time. Mr. Volpi, after sleeping soundly for nearly ten hours, returned to his post that evening feeling a new man.

As was the procedure, the First Purser advised him and the returned Miss Gonzales of all the current problems of the day. They included a lost stroller, two missing credit cards and a faxed police report from Los Angeles, to be read at their convenience. The First Purser officially turned the office over to them and left.

It was the police report that drained the color from Mr. Volpi's face, causing him to seek the stability of the nearest chair before he fell down. He read the report twice before actually absorbing it. Then he emptied the trash can upside down and tore through the contents, only to sigh and return to his chair.

He looked so stunned that the recently divorced Miss Gonzales, who couldn't stand him but had often used his desire for her to her own advantage, took the report from his trembling hand.

In a concerned voice, she read aloud in perfect English, with only a slight Spanish accent. A scholarship to the University of Mexico in English studies served her well.

"Wanted for questioning in connection with the death and robbery of the eighty-seven year old California Cheddar Cheese Heiress, Margaret Rawlins, is her attendant, Ms. Coral Barker. Ms. Barker vanished on September 15th, the day Miss Rawlins was discovered bludgeoned to death. Missing are the legendary "Eye of the Peacock" jewels, which are comprised of a matching necklace, earrings, and cocktail ring made of flawless opals, sapphires, and diamonds. According to the famous jewelers, Van Cleef and Arpel's, the set, once purported to belong to Mrs. Wallace Simpson, is valued at over two million dollars."

Miss Gonzales heard a strangled cry come from Mr. Volpi. She glanced at him anxiously before continuing to read in her soothing, contralto voice.

"Ms. Barker has possibly left the country under an assumed name. All airports, bus terminals, train stations, and cruise lines should be on the alert. The Rawlins family is offering a fifty thousand dollar reward for any information on Ms. Barker's whereabouts, as well as a two-hundred thousand dollar reward for the return of the jewels. Below is an artist's rendering of the distinctive design of the jewelry. No likeness of Coral Barker is available."

Miss Gonzales stopped reading and looked at Mr. Volpi over the top of the paper, whose face had turned decidedly ashen.

It was the artist's rendering of the ring that moments before had completely undone Mr. Volpi. It looked exactly like the ring he'd cavalierly thrown into the trashcan the night before. While Mr. Volpi sat there shaking and in shock, Miss Gonzales voiced a concern that he might be suffering from the same flu-like symptoms she endured only the night before.

She sweetly offered to cover for him, as he had done so many times for her, and begged him to go to bed. Finally able to stand, he agreed and staggered back to his cabin. Miss Gonzales watched him totter down the hallway and out of sight before she made a quick phone call.

* * * *

Alone in the cabin he shared with an entertainer who, mercifully, was playing the piano and singing in one of the many lounges until three or four in the morning, Mr. Volpi retrieved a hidden flask. He poured himself a large drink and tried to think. Talking out loud had always helped him put his thoughts in order in the past.

"All right, Victor Volpi. You are in big, big trouble. Not only have you missed the opportunity to get a reward, but you will probably lose your job for throwing that ring away."

He took a slug of the whisky and chewed his lower lip. Thinking was not one of his strengths but he knew the ring was already destroyed.

The days were gone when most ships threw flotsam and jetsam overboard a few times a week. According to international law they still could, but as with most major cruise lines, all debris aboard the Galaxy Cruise Ships was separated and compacted daily within the ship's sophisticated recycling center.

The compacted trash is stored and then, at no insignificant expense, sent to a landfill upon the return of the ship to the home base. Even if he told the authorities what he had done, the ring had already been crushed beyond recognition and buried between tons of garbage.

His career, which was already faltering due to an incident involving a young female passenger, would be crushed, as well. He would have been First Purser instead of Second, if it hadn't been for that groping incident, he thought bitterly.

Another thought came into his head. Did the discovery of the ring mean the companion, Coral Barker, was aboard ship? Probably. Did Mr. Volpi care? Hell, no. Better he should stay out of this.

"All right. So you've blown the chance to make some easy money. What's done is done. What you've got to do now is make sure the steward, what's her name, doesn't tell anyone about the ring. That's all you need. What was her name? It was Polish or something. Lillian, Lorraine, Lucille. No, no." He became disgusted with himself.

"Those aren't Polish names, you jerk. Wait! Lu-sa! That's it. Lusa something or other." Mr. Volpi stood up and started pacing his small quarters.

"I'll check the roster for her name and see where her cabin is. I'll make her promise to keep her mouth shut or I'll shut it for her." For one moment Mr. Volpi's face looked cruel and ugly, a side only very few unfortunate people saw.

* * * *

Lusa had worked hard all day but, while descending the stairs to her small cabin on the lower deck, she had come up with a plan. She was not an educated woman, but she was bright, energetic and well liked.

She would go to her fellow stewards and seek their help. When you work as hard as they did and in such a close environment, there is an intense camaraderie. She knew they would understand her dilemma.

She had been a fool to go to her betters; her friends would help her. She would find the owner and this weight would be lifted from her shoulders.

Still deep in thought, Lusa wandered into a starboard section of the ship she normally had little reason to visit and rounded a corner. She collided with a woman, a woman smaller than even she, who was hurrying around the same corner from the other side.

Lusa nearly knocked the woman over. She made a grab for her, filled with apologies, when she saw the sparkle on her ears.

"What is this that I see?" Lusa, a deeply religious woman, began to praise God's ways loudly in her native tongue.

The woman looked at her with fearful, wide opened eyes. "What....what do you want? Who are you? Who are you?"

"I am Lyudmila Bostranovich, but please to call me Lusa." She pointed to the earrings on the other woman's ears.

"I see the earrings. I have found you!"

As Lusa reached into her pocket to return the ring, the woman backed up shrieking. She ripped the earrings from her ears and flung them at Lusa.

One earring went over Lusa's head and the other hit her below the right eye, sharp prongs cutting into her face. Lusa cried out in pain, lost her balance and fell to the floor.

Dazed, she watched the woman run down the corridor, round another turn and disappear. When she caught her breath, Lusa got up, picked up the earrings, put them into the pocket with the ring and went to her cabin, where she applied Neosporin to her wound.

* * * *

Mr. Volpi knocked on Lusa's door on Deck One, aft, glancing furtively around him. So far, the corridors were clear. When she answered the door, his plan was to frighten her into keeping quiet about the ring.

He wasn't above a little physical persuasion, as anyone who knew him intimately could tell you, but he would wait to see if that was necessary. No one answered. After checking once again to make sure the corridor was still clear, he opened the door with a stolen passkey.

Within moments he ascertained the tiny room was empty, left, and renewed his search for the steward. He only had tonight to make sure she didn't talk. Tomorrow, someone might tell her about the faxed police report. News traveled fast on a ship. Now where did she say she found that ring, anyway? Mr. Volpi hurried along.

* * * *

Lusa, upon returning to her cabin and seeing the cut on her face in the mirror, thought the ship's doctor should take a look at it. Consequently, she was not in her room when sought out by Volpi, but returning from the medical center, Deck One, forward.

Doctor Grant had wisely put a small retaining bandage on the cut to minimize any scarring. When asked how it happened, Lusa decided telling the truth, especially with three pieces of someone else's jewelry in her pocket, might get her into trouble.

Lying didn't come easily to her, but it was her only option. The doctor, who had his hands full dealing with the dislocated knee of a sixteen-year old boy and his emotionally charged parents, only half-listened to her story about a fall onto a piece of broken glass, anyway.

It was now ten-thirty pm and the Captain's Luau on the tenth floor, Lido Deck, was in full swing. This gala event was highly popular with the passengers and most of them were attending the function, leaving much of the rest of the ship deserted.

Avoiding what few stray guests there were, Lusa slowly climbed the stairs from the first level to the Promenade, level three. She found herself standing in front of the same stairway where she'd found the ring the day before.

Lusa sighed and wondered what she had done to cause the woman to run away. Lusa had to admit, her accent was heavy and sometimes hard to understand. And she was almost yelling at the woman. But did she act so strangely it should have frightened the woman like that?

Puzzled by the passenger's behavior, she felt something was not quite right. Maybe it was time to talk to her supervisor and hand the jewels over to the head steward. She was tired of the burden and her wounded cheek throbbed. Turning to go to bed, Lusa heard quiet sobbing in the darkness not more than twenty feet away from her, near the outside railing.

There was no moon this evening and the deck, well lit at the steps, was much dimmer nearer the sea. Lusa squinted in the gloom and saw a small woman, clutching a small box in one of her hands and crying quietly into the other. A person of caring and sympathy, Lusa was torn between leaving the woman to her privacy and asking if she could be of help.

That was before the woman saw Lusa standing in the light near the staircase. The woman let out a shriek instantly recognizable to the steward. Her mouth open, Lusa stood frozen to the spot, as the woman began a combination of crying and hurling accusations at her.

"You! Can't you leave me alone? I didn't mean to do it. It was an accident. She found me trying on her jewelry and slapped me. I didn't mean to hit her with the paperweight but I'd had enough. That miserable old woman was hateful to me for years, so I kept hitting her and hitting her until I couldn't hit her any more. But it was an accident. I didn't mean to kill her."

"But the ring..." said Lusa moving closer, only to be interrupted by the hysterical woman.

"I lost the ring! It was too big and it came off my finger. I didn't mean to lose it. Why are you torturing me like this? Haven't I been through enough?" The woman screamed as she backed up even closer to the railing.

"Here! Here! Take the necklace. Take it. I never want to see any of those jewels again." And with that, the woman threw the slender box at Lusa with such force she instinctively caught it, as one would catch a football.

"I…I.." said Lusa, only to feel a painful blow to the back of her head.

Ms. Barker watched in horror as Lusa crumpled to the deck, and a man in a white uniform came out of the shadows, threw down a fire extinguisher, and ran toward her. Panicking, Ms. Barker climbed the railing to escape the lunatic who was rushing at her, surely to do her bodily harm.

Mr. Volpi did not think about what he looked like to Ms. Barker as he lunged for her. All he could think about was whatever reward he could get for the return of the necklace. He would lie about the ring. In fact, he instantly knew he would lie about the steward's part in this; somehow make her out as one of the villains. After all, she was only a simple immigrant from a backwater country.

Here was his ticket to a bright, new future. He would capture this murderess, turn her over to the authorities and become a hero. Maybe he would make First Purser, after all.

All these thoughts tumbled through his mind, as he grabbed the woman around the waist and tried to pull her off the railing. Ms. Barker fought with all her might, ascending higher and higher and Mr. Volpi followed, determined to keep her from getting away.

Like many small, wiry people, Ms. Barker was stronger than she seemed. She grabbed Mr. Volpi around the neck in a strangle hold and pulled him off balance. With a shocked look on both their faces, they fell, not onto a deck below, but as they were at the widest part of the ship, into the inky, black waters of the Pacific Ocean.

Miss Gonzales, who had been momentarily paralyzed by all that was happening, surfaced from her hiding place. She had been following Mr. Volpi, and now raced to the nearby signal box. Using her key, she sounded the ship-wide, six-digit code for "man overboard," which could be heard throughout the vessel.

Instantly, she felt the subtle lurch of the liner's powerful engines go into a full reversal. Knowing they would still travel one or two more miles depending on the currents, Miss Gonzales ran to the railing, where she'd seen the two fall into the ocean.

Miss Gonzales raised a stiff arm. As every member of the crew was instructed to do, she pointed like a hunting dog to the spot and remained there awaiting further instructions.

She was concerned about the steward lying unconscious on the deck, but knew her job was to point and stare without moving. Soon the recovery team would come to her for a positioning, even though she could see nothing in the moonless night sky but an enormous, black void.

In less than ninety seconds she heard electronic pulleys lowering a powerful speedboat into the water. The Staff First Officer, head of the Search and Rescue Team, arrived and ask her taut questions, which he relayed through his walkie-talkie to the speedboat.

Miss Gonzales remained in her frozen position, as is required, until the officer commanded her to stand down. In less than five minutes the well-trained crew was in the water and searching with flares, while the luxury liner floated listless in the ocean.

* * * *

Lusa tried to open her eyes. She moaned and felt someone take her hand and stroke it soothingly.

She thought she could distinguish a familiar voice with a Spanish accent. It sounded like Miss Gonzales, whom she knew vaguely.

Occasionally they spoke about the two children left behind while each mother was forced to make a living. But why would the Purser be on deck with her and why did her head ache so?

When she was able to open her eyes, she saw she was not on deck but back in the medical center. She groggily focused in on Miss Gonzales, Doctor Grant, and the captain of the ship, who were smiling down at her.

"What happened?" she managed to ask in a raspy voice. She was still in her uniform, but the top of her head was covered with gauze.

"Shhhh," said Miss Gonzales. "Don't speak, *pobrecita*, just rest."

Lusa tried to raise her head from the pillow.

"Now, don't move, Lusa," said the doctor kindly. "I've been seeing a lot of you this evening! You're going to be fine, but you need to take it easy for the next couple of days."

"But what has happened?" Lusa demanded, touching her head cautiously. "Someone tell me." She stared at Captain Yurman, whose red face and bushy white eyebrows reminded her of *Ded Moroz*, the Slavic version of Santa Claus.

Captain Yurman cleared his throat. "Mrs. Bostranovich, I hardly know where to begin, but I wanted to be the one to tell you, personally. I don't want you to hear it from anyone else."

He hesitated then went on. "You were struck on the head with a fire extinguisher by Mr. Volpi, who will pay for his crimes to the fullest extent of the law, should we find him. You are going to be all right but he and Ms. Barker went overboard and are presumed dead, thanks to that madman."

"You were lucky Volpi didn't hit you harder," interjected Doctor Grant, "and that Miss Gonzales found you right away. It could have been a lot more serious."

"She was there to sound the alarm so we could, at least, attempt a rescue," said the captain. "Thanks to Miss Gonzales, we know everything that happened or at least her version." He gestured to the smiling Hispanic woman, who sat down on the bed beside Lusa. "Now we must know what *you* have to say. This is a very serious matter."

Miss Gonzales leaned in. "*Si*, I told them everything, but they must hear it from you, too."

Lusa looked from one to the other. "Everything? I --"

The captain interrupted, saying, "Miss Gonzales told us you were attempting to retrieve the necklace from Ms. Barker to return it to its rightful owners. Purser Volpi struck you down and tried to steal it for himself." A highly agitated Captain Yurman turned to the doctor.

"You know, I did not pick that man. He was already assigned to this ship when I took over command. The responsibility for his behavior lies strictly on the previous captain's shoulders."

"If you say so," muttered Jeremiah Grant.

"They are…overboard?" Lusa asked in a daze.

"We will, of course, continue the search but it has been nearly three hours and both are probably drowned," continued Captain Yurman. "These are treacherous waters. Meanwhile, we have confirmed that while the woman was registered onboard as Ms. Cora Parker, she was, in reality, a Ms. Coral Barker. The birth certificate she used to get aboard ship was altered but upon closer inspection, you could see where she changed the name."

"You need to check those things more carefully in the future," the doctor chided, thrusting an old-fashioned thermometer into Lusa's mouth.

"Yes, well," Captain Yurman's face reddened a shade darker and he went on quickly, "She is – or was -- wanted for questioning in the murder of Margaret Rawlins, but you already knew that, you clever woman, you."

He beamed warmly at Lusa, who stared up at him.

"You are one of the recent hires, right? Brought on during my command, right?"

The doctor rolled his eyes but said nothing.

"*Si*, Capitan, as am I," said Miss Gonzales before Lusa could speak. "I am so glad that I was suspicious of *Señor* Volpi's behavior and arranged for someone to take over my station tonight so I could follow him. When I did so, I was able to see and hear everything."

Lusa stared at her and gurgled.

"I saw how brave you were, *mi amiga*," Miss Gonzales said, looking directly at Lusa. "Your daughter will be proud."

"I? Brave?" Lusa said, nearly biting the thermometer in half.

"Oh, yes," said the captain with pride.

"We've heard all about it from Miss Gonzales, and now that you've confirmed it, please do not tax yourself further, Mrs. Bostranovich. The Galaxy Cruise Lines and I will be eternally grateful for your efforts. "

The Captain shook his head in disbelief.

"To think that one of my crewmembers attempted to murder you and succeeded in killing himself and one of the passengers. I cannot believe that lunatic was under my command! Thank God I did not hire him," he added quickly.

"You're still going to have a lot to answer for," Dr. Grant mused aloud.

"Oh, shut up," Captain Yurman snapped, rocking back and forth on his heels.

The doctor shrugged, removing the thermometer from Lisa's mouth. He studied the results. Lusa tried to make sense of it all.

"I do not understand. I want only to give the lady --"

"*Pobrecita!*" Miss Gonzales interrupted and turned to the two men. "See how the blow on the head, *señors*, has temporarily erased her memory? You remember the reward, Mrs. Bostranovich, don't you? We spoke of the reward earlier this evening, when you said you might know where the necklace was and who had it. That was right after we were talking about how much you missed your Natasha and I, my Carlos."

What Lusa knew was that they had not exchanged anything other than a "good evening" for several days. Her mind raced, the doctor fussed with her chart, and the captain paced back and forth.

Miss Gonzales took Lusa's hand again and said, "I've explained to Captain Yurman and the doctor how I witnessed you trying to talk the woman into turning herself in to the authorities. How you tried to do what was right."

Miss Gonzales' eyes twinkled at Lusa's confusion.

"Otherwise, they would not have known about what the wicked Victor Volpi did. They might have thought you were actually stealing the necklace or had something to do with those two falling overboard." Miss Gonzales' beautiful features became hard.

Lusa drew in a sharp breath.

Watching Lusa's every move, Miss Gonzales, went on easily, "*Si*, but do not worry. I am your witness. I heard you plead with the murderess to turn herself in. I saw the terrible Mr. Volpi strike you. That is why you deserve the fifty thousand dollar reward for finding Ms. Barker, and that is why I help you."

"And then, of course, there's the reward for the return of the jewelry," threw in the Doctor. "No paltry sum of money."

"You remember the reward for the return of the jewelry, don't you?" Miss Gonzales stoked Lusa's hand.

Lusa shook her head with care.

"I'm sure the family will give you part of the reward for the return of the necklace, as well as the fifty thousand dollars for the information on Ms. Barker," said Doctor Grant, straightening bottles of medication in a cabinet. "I know I would."

"It's too bad about the missing earrings and ring," said Miss Gonzales, with a frown.

"No, the ring, I have it. And the earrings, too. Here," Lusa said, reaching inside her pocket and pulled out the three dazzling pieces. "But I did nothing to ---"

"*Capitan!*" interrupted Miss. Gonzales again, the excitement in her voice overriding that of Lusa's protestation.

"Look what Mrs. Bostranovich has. She never ceases to amaze us." Miss Gonzales pointed to the hand containing the sparkling gems, while warmly squeezing the wounded woman's other.

"Well, I'll be. If you're not a wonder, Mrs. Bostranovich," Captain Yurman boomed appreciatively.

"This is good news! The company will be very happy about this, as am I. With the help of Miss Gonzales' testimony, I'm sure you will not only receive the reward for information leading to the whereabouts of Ms. Barker, but also the two-hundred thousand dollar reward for the return of all the jewelry. This can ensure my pension, if I handle it correctly," the captain said, lost in thought.

"Now you're thinking," said the doctor.

"They might give to me all that money? I can go home?" Lusa could hardly believe her ears.

"After all," Captain Yurman said, "I cannot be responsible for another man's hire but I can take care of my own people."

"Well said," the doctor commented, as the infirmary phone rang.

Doctor Grant answered the call, speaking quietly into the phone. The captain preened, and straightened a black and white photo of the ship hanging lopsided on the wall.

Miss Gonzales sighed softly. "I am so happy for you, *señora*. If only I had enough money to return to my little one. His grandmother cares for him deeply but a five-year old child needs his mother, don't you think? With a little more in my savings, I could work part-time in Mexico City and be with my son. It is something I wish for more than anything else in the world. But I am happy that what I *said* I saw and heard will help you return to your child."

Both women locked eyes, just as the captain turned his attention back to Lusa lying in the hospital bed.

"Mrs. Bostranovich, if everything happened as you say, and Miss Gonzales verifies, there should be no problem in getting you the full two-hundred and fifty thousand dollars. In fact, I'll see to it," Captain Yurman said firmly. "We will be sorry to lose you, but money like that will go a long way in the Ukraine."

Miss Gonzales smiled down at Lusa. "Yes. As in my country, even half would be a small fortune."

"Half?" Lusa looked at Miss Gonzales.

"*Si*. Half of two-hundred and fifty thousand dollars is one hundred and twenty-five thousand American dollars. If I had such a sum, it would allow me to stay home with my son, just as it would allow you to be home with your daughter."

"Yes, I see." Lusa touched her head. "I am not thinking so fast."

She looked away from the second purser to the captain of the Galaxy Star, elsewhere in his thoughts.

"Captain Yurman, Miss Gonzales can share with me the reward? My life she saves. And she was much…much… what is the word?"

"Help?" Miss Gonzales offered.

"Yes, help to me. Please say she can have the half."

"Of course," said the Captain in surprise, now focusing his attention on the two women. "You are free to do whatever you want with the money. If you want to split it with your friend that is your right."

"My right, yes. To split."

"Then it is done," said the captain with authority.

"Good man," said the doctor, hanging up the phone and clapping the captain on the back.

He had only been half listening to the conversation in the room, but felt he got the gist of it. He stretched up and whispered into the taller man's ear, "I think you just pulled this out of the fire. The women sharing the reward is even better publicity."

"It is, isn't it?" the Captain whispered back. He turned to Lusa and Miss Gonzales.

"Don't you worry. I will take care of everything. But for now, I should return to the helm. I have a ship to run."

He strode to the door, pulled it open, and left with a flourish. The doctor watched him leave.

"Always the ham that one." He turned to the two women.

"I will leave you ladies to each other's company, as well. That phone call was from the parents of a sixteen-year old boy, who I need to attend to in their stateroom."

He crossed to the door.

"Don't stay too long, Miss Gonzales. Lusa needs her rest. But if you want anything, just ring for the nurse outside."

"Thank you," the women said in unison, and watched the door close behind him. Miss Gonzales looked at Lusa for a moment before speaking.

"Before I leave, Mrs. Bostranovich, I want to say you're English may not be good, together we make *buena fortuna* happen." The Hispanic woman saw confusion spread on Lusa's face. "'The phrase means good fortune in Spanish."

Lusa nodded, comprehending. "In my language we say *Ščasty vam/tobi*, Miss Gonzales."

"You must call me Raquel, Mrs. Bostranovich." The 'r' rolled softly from Miss Gonzales' tongue, as she spoke her name. "For I will never forget your generosity."

"Oh, no, Raquel. It is only as it should be. And please to call me Lusa."

Encounter
A Short Story
by
Heather Haven

Encounter

Mrs. Everett Wolcott walked inside the glass doors of the small but exclusive department store. She straightened her back, as her brigadier general father had taught her, and stretched to her full height of five foot, four inches, with the help of her four-inch Prada heels.

One hand smoothed the cashmere of her hot pink and mandarin orange two-piece suit, created for her by an up and coming Santa Fe Designer. The other stroked the lustrous fur of the sable scarf jauntily tossed around her shoulders.

She posed for any admiring glances from customers and staff. None forthcoming, she relaxed and breathed in air laced with the scent of expensive perfumes and fine leather.

The upper classes still hold on to a few things, she thought.

The special ordered twelve-hundred dollar shoes from Italy had arrived. The staff was very anxious for her to try them on to see if they were acceptable or should be returned to Florence. If everything went as usual, six people would attend her every need until she finally deemed the shoes worthy. Mrs. Wolcott was content.

Allison Jenkins leaned against the countertop, the pink slip clutched in her hand. Her mind raced. One customer complaint and she was fired. They didn't even have the guts to tell her in person, other than her boss dropping by to instruct her to clean out her locker at the end of the day. After two years of hard work.

And here I thought I had a shot at a new job; a step up.

They'd added some comment about her coming back ten-minutes late from lunch. But she'd had to pick up the cake for her daughter's eighth birthday and couldn't do it after work. Her daughter's school let out only fifteen minutes after she finished her job. If Allison didn't pick her up on time, she'd be charged one dollar for every minute the teacher was kept waiting. The cake was supposed to be a happy surprise. Allison felt the room spin. Then her face hardened.

It wasn't the tardiness. It was the complaint. I never get a break.

Mrs. Wolcott walked to the cosmetics counter, her heels clicking against the floor. She threw her errant sable scarf over her left shoulder clipping Allison, who was still leaning against the counter in a daze, on the forehead. Mrs. Wolcott watched the flutter of soft, fine hair go awry and cast the young woman a beneficent smile.

Allison drew in a ragged breath, tried to return the smile, and gave her attention to the difficult customer she'd waited on countless times before.

What's it like to have all that money? It's like you're from another planet.

Wordless, Mrs. Wolcott pointed to a skin toner on the second shelf and then glanced appraisingly at her nails, her thoughts drifting to the demands of the evening.

Time for another manicure. You'd think they'd last more than a week but that's the kind of shoddy service you get nowadays from these foreigners. I should probably have a pedicure, too. I'll drop by the salon on my way home and they'd better be able to fit me in after all the business I've given them. How dreary, but I must look my best for Babs' cocktail party tonight. And my Versace, of course. The green one. Babs will be green with envy when she sees how thin I look in it. It's delicious.

Mrs. Wolcott caught the reflection of her face in a three-quarter profile in a small, round mirror on the counter. She was pleased with what she saw. The last trip to Switzerland was nothing short of miraculous, although with the last facelift and skin peel, her skin was more sensitive than ever. Still, she didn't look a day over forty-five. Not that sixty-four is old. Well, sixty-seven, actually, but that's not old.

She drew her attention back to Allison, bending down to take the wrong bottle from the bottom shelf.

"No, no. Not that one," Mrs. Wolcott said in annoyance. "Why would I use something like that? Do you think I have the skin of rhinoceros? I have very sensitive skin, prone to melanoma. So for God's sake, be careful. The one next to it and please hurry up. I haven't got all day."

"I'm sorry, ma'am. I misunderstood." Allison straightened up and set a slim, lavender bottle on the counter.

Mrs. Wolcott picked it up, glanced at the label, and set it back down on the counter. "Yes, that's it. Please have it sent to my home. You have the address for Mrs. Everett Wolcott?"

"Yes, ma'am, we have your card on file. Will that be cash or charge?"

"Well, charge, of course. Just put it on my account. My goodness, how many times do I have to tell you people something like that? Didn't you wait on me yesterday and several times before that? I had to complain about you then."

"You complained about me?"

"And not for the first time." Mrs. Wolcott sniffed. "I suppose standards have become lax these days. My father, the Brigadier General, would not have accepted such behaviour within the ranks."

"You're the one." Allison spoke in barely a whisper, staring at the thin, older woman.

"Ninety-seven and going strong," said Mrs. Wolcott, removing a silk hanky from her sleeve and dabbing at her nose. Mrs. Wolcott offered the stunned, younger woman a coral-lipsticked smile, framed by perfectly matching white teeth. "As I've said many times before, the world would do well to emulate the General."

Allison came to life.

"The General? Brigadier General Harold Wilson? Over at Shady Nook Rest Home? Of course! That's your father. My friend, Patty, works there and we've talked about you regularly showing up at my counter."

Her eyes began to glitter with an inside fire, as realization paved every oncoming word.

"In fact, Patty messaged me he got loose the other day and was found walking down the street with his dong hanging out. She thought I would be interested. Your dad's supposed to be a regular old letch. The police were called and everything."

"Why, that's an outrageous thing to say." Mrs. Wolcott sputtered. "It was a mistake. Some unsavory person said he revealed himself. It's not true."

"I heard full frontal nudity." Allison let out a hoot of laughter. "You know, I'm surprised it's not all over the internet, what with him being a retired Brigadier General. And you being a robber baron's wife." She paused. "Whoops! Did I say that? I mean a real estate mogul's wife. And such a big deal in our community. Well, these things happen. Just like being fired."

"You watch your tone, young lady. You cannot speak to me that way. And keep your voice down." Mrs. Wolcott stuttered for a moment then reclaimed herself. "The person who said that is no longer employed at the rest home."

"Really? Well, aren't you a busy little bee?" Allison pseudo-whispering in return, leaned on the counter with a bright smile. "But it still happened, lady, no matter how many people you get fired."

"There's no proof."

"But there is! Patty took a picture with her phone. She managed to get a shot before they subdued him. She attached it to a text message she sent me. I think I've still got it."

Allison reached down and brought out her handbag. She pulled out her phone. Mrs. Wolcott blinked and hyperventilated. Allison scrolled through a set of images and settled on one.

"Ah! Yes, here it is. Crystal clear, too. Excellent shot. You can't fault these phones for clarity. There's his face…and…ah ….everything."

The salesgirl turned the phone around so the woman could see the shot. After her initial shock, Mrs. Wolcott made a lunge for the phone. Allison deflected and spun away with glee.

"You know, I'm going to be honest with you, Mrs. Wolcott. If you're going to admit to having a ninety-seven year old father, it's time to stop the facelifts. Besides, you've had so many, I'll bet that dimple in your chin is really your belly button."

"How dare you!" Mrs. Wolcott's voice rose to a piercing pitch. Looking around, she lowered it again, making her tone soft but menacing. "Alva, isn't it? Or Alice? I am going to --"

"Have me fired? Too late. You already did that. And it's Allison. Not Alva, Alice or Alexander the Great. Although at the moment, I'm feeling a little bit like a conqueror. All I need is an elephant. Or was that Hannibal? My daughter would know. I'll have to ask her."

Allison picked up her handbag. "Well, I think we're done here. You had me fired, so I may as well leave."She waved her phone in front of the older woman.

"But what to do with this picture of the General? It hadn't dawned on me until now that this could be a real photo op. I could text some of my friends. Or better yet, put it on the internet. Share it with the world at large."

"Don't do that. Please don't do that." Mrs. Wolcott's voice was beseeching. "Please."

"Why shouldn't I? Tell me that?"

Mrs. Wolcott licked dry lips. Allison watched the woman. Her demeanor became that of a small child caught by her elders, searching for a way to get out of a spanking. Then Mrs. Wolcott spoke softly, almost to herself.

"I could go upstairs, talk to personnel. That would do it, wouldn't it, Al….?" Mrs. Wolcott hesitated again over the name.

"Allison," the younger woman offered with a chuckle. "You should try to remember people's names. It doesn't take much, really, just paying attention to someone else for a change."

"Allison. Yes, Allison. I'll tell them I was mistaken. Make them give you your job back. I can do that. They'll listen to me. My husband owns a percentage of the store."

"Does he?" Allison stared at her with new appreciation. "Well, isn't that lovely? That means you can get me my job back with a raise."

"I could. And a promotion. There's an opening for a new cosmetics' buyer," Mrs. Wolcott added with eagerness. Now she was the small child going for an 'A'.

"I know. I applied for that position last week, but they haven't made a decision yet."

"It's yours, Allison. You'll see. Only promise me…" she broke off, looking at the younger woman with pleading eyes. It was Allison's turn to smile beneficently.

"My mother always taught me that one good turn deserves another. Don't you worry; you do your part and I'll do mine."

"Yes, yes. Good." Relief flooded through Mrs. Wolcott's being. "Thank you."

"You're welcome." Allison's voice contained a touch of mockery, unnoticed by Mrs. Wolcott. "Time for you to zip upstairs and get me that job. You've got one hour before I do some serious internet stuff."

Her face took on a smile as hard as chiseled stone. This did not go unnoticed by Mrs. Wolcott.

"Yes, yes, of course," she stuttered. Mrs. Wolcott pivoted and moved toward the elevators only to be stopped by Allison's raised voice.

"One more thing."

Mrs. Wolcott spun around and obediently ran back to the counter. Once there, Allison crooked her finger, signaling Mrs. Wolcott to lean closer. Mrs. Wolcott leaned in for all she was worth.

"I had a thought," Allison whispered. "While you're straightening out messes, call up the nursing home and tell them to give my friend, Patty, her job back. She's got three kids to feed."

"I'll see what I can do…Allison," Mrs. Wolcott added the salesgirl's name for emphasis.

"You're going to do more than that. She's got the picture, too. She's the one who texted me with it. Remember that."

The color drained from the socialite's face. "Yes, I'd forgotten."

"And here's your face astringent. Take it with you, like everyone else does. It only weighs three ounces."

Allison pressed the small bottle into Mrs. Wolcott's hand. The older woman tottered, her other hand reaching out to the countertop for support.

"Off you go, Mrs. Wolcott. Time's a wasting. Have personnel call me when this has been straightened out. I'll be down here waiting."

Mrs. Wolcott nodded, straightened her posture, as her Brigadier General father had taught her, and walked to the elevators. As Allison watched the back of her disappear behind closing doors she mused, looking down at her phone.

When my daughter gets old enough to have a phone, I'm going to let her text all she wants.

Jemma and the Shoe
A Short Story
by
Heather Haven

Jemma and the Shoe

It was midnight and Mrs. Rappaport sat with the German pistol in her lap, loaded and ready to go. It would get going shortly. This was the night she was going to do it and with her father's fine example of World War II weaponry. Even though Mrs. Rappaport had not slept for nearly twenty-four hours, she went over her plan again and again.

Her husband's upcoming demise had nothing to do with him being with other women, running his business into the ground, or his gambling debts, although these did not make her happy. No, it was the fact he'd looted her own beloved business, an antique store that gave her life meaning. How could he think she wouldn't notice his substituting a bad reproduction for the Early American "Eye of the Boar" roadhouse sign, circa 1793, worth sixteen-thousand dollars? Absurd.

The disposal of his body would take place on top of a plateau on a steep hill in an adjoining park. The tree-covered plateau butted up against their backyard and never had anyone on it. It was a perfect place to get rid of the body, because that was the rub, she thought shrewdly, how to get rid of the body.

At one fifty-nine a.m. the front door opened. A well-aimed shot was fired. Mrs. Rappaport's plan took shape.

* * * *

At six-thirty a.m., as was the custom, Jemma Marie Zenbull of Belgium, an English bulldog known for her good-nature and sweetness, trotted through the neighborhood on her powerful short legs toward the park. Jemma loved her twice a day visits to the park. The morning air was cool and crisp and promised much. In the evenings, the park smelled of the sun and all the visitors it had seen through the day. The evening walks were a little shorter than the morning's but just as enjoyable to her.

For nearly seven years, Jemma had been pampered, adored, coddled, kissed, hugged, and fussed over. But she was about to dash up a small, plateaued hill and all that would change.

Ever since her owners saw that the hill was fenced on the far side and felt no harm could come to their beloved pet, they released her leash and let her run up to the plateau as fast as her short legs would take her. This was her ten or fifteen-minutes of total freedom, a chance to be herself. She could stop where she wanted, say hello to flowers, insects, squirrels, and, just possibly, roll around on some lovely, questionable mound of something.

Her female owner unhooked the leash the base of the hill with the words, "All right, Jemma. You can go now."

Jemma scrambled around to the side and up the narrow path she had traversed many times, a path unknown to anyone save Jemma and her owners. This unseen path had sturdy roots, small ridges and deep rock formations that was used for the secure placement of thick paws, as she placed them now, scampering up the almost forty-five degree incline.

Once at the top, she would have a brief rest. It was tradition. Then, after a bit, Jemma would sniff around the bushes, grass, and trees, in her search for anything new and fun. Snorting loudly and trying to catch her breath, she padded to the center of the plateau, splayed herself down on the cool grass, and sniffed the air appreciatively.

As she did so, some surprising new scents greeted her. First, there was the scent of a human nearby, puzzling to Jemma, as it did not quite smell the way she was used to humans smelling. Second, was the aroma of fine leather, a fragrance near and dear to Jemma's heart.

Jemma, as previously stated, was a wondrous, beauteous bulldog, and her virtues were oft sung far and wide, but she had one tiny, little flaw - leather. Her owners finally resorted to putting their shoes out of her reach, particularly after she ate a pair of her female owner's three-hundred dollar Ferragamo heels. Consequently, Jemma had not had the taste of good leather for quite a while.

Jemma got up and walked over to where the two smells converged and saw that they were attached to one another. She grunted for a moment, accessing the situation and rightly concluded that this male human was not quite himself. Jemma had found a gopher like this once and knew instinctively the gopher would not be getting up and going about his business anytime soon. So, as only a really intelligent animal can do at such a time, she shrugged and moved down the body to the second and most interesting smell.

There, on each foot and giving off a delectable aroma, were exceptionally fine Italian loafers complete with fringed tassels. Jemma knew tassels were the tastiest part of any shoe and rarely, if ever, seen by her. She grabbed at one only to hear a well-known voice.

"Jemma! Come on, girl. Come on down. I have to go to work, sweetie."

Jemma froze with the tassel in her mouth. Then she dropped the morsel and looked toward the sound of her mistress's voice.

A finger was removed from the trigger of a pistol aimed at Jemma's head.

"Jemma! Jemma," came a sterner command. "Come down here this minute."

Jemma grunted with disappointment and took a step or two toward the voice.

The pistol lowered.

With a sad snort, Jemma glanced back at the tasseled loafer and then dashed down the hill toward her waiting owner.

Mrs. Rappaport, pistol in hand and perspiring profusely, stepped out from behind the thick pine tree some thirty feet away. She looked at Mr. Rappaport, half hidden in the brush, and wiped the sweat from her burning eyes.

"Where the hell did that animal come from? I've been watching this place for weeks. I thought it was inaccessible except from our yard. Oh, God, it's beginning to get light," she said, already exhausted from her murderous ordeal. "I've got to hide you better," she muttered, as she dragged the body deeper into the brush.

"I'll be back tonight, when it gets dark. I'll bury you and be rid of you, finally! And I'd better not see that stupid mutt again, either."

* * * *

It was early evening and Jemma sat by the front door eyeing her leash. Yes, she had been let out into the backyard to relieve herself when her owners came home, but it wasn't the same. After dinner and before everyone settled in for the evening, Jemma would have her walk.

She heard the lower, male voice talking to her. "Ready to go for your walk, Jemma?"

As her limited vocabulary did include the word "walk," she leapt up, sneezed in her excitement as bulldogs often do, and nuzzled her leash. Off they went in their familiar routine. At the bottom of the small hill, Jemma scooted up the side and ran directly to the ex-human and his tasseled shoes.

Yes, he was a little further back in the brush, but his smell was riper now, which made the shoes all the more alluring. Without hesitation, Jemma grabbed the heel of one.

"Drop that shoe, you disgusting animal!" the woman growled softly but with a fierceness that made Jemma freeze.

She didn't recognize the woman's voice but she did know the three words "drop that shoe," so she obeyed. She also knew the difference in vocal tones and this voice was full of rage, an emotion never before expressed toward our Jemma.

Her ears raised and she looked at the woman coming at her out of the gloom carrying something unfamiliar in her hands. It was a shovel and the woman was holding it like a baseball bat.

"Jemma! Come on, Girl. Time to go home. Time for bed," the voice of her master sang out to her, warm and loving. Jemma turned and dashed toward the familiar voice, and so intent was she, she didn't see or sense the swinging piece of metal that missed her hindquarters by mere inches.

Mrs. Rappaport stood on the hill furious and determined. She had no intention of letting a dog interfere with her plan. She had worked too hard and there was too much at stake. She tried to contain her panic by telling herself that once she buried Mr. Rappaport, the dog would either lose interest or wouldn't be able to find the body. Content in her ignorance, she began to dig.

She found the ground a little harder than she thought, due to a lack of rain for the past several weeks. Even though she worked through much of the night, the grave was shallower than she originally planned it to be. But then Mrs. Rappaport noticed, nothing was going quite the way she'd planned.

* * * *

The next morning Jemma raced up the hill and could not believe her good fortune. She found the ever-ripening body instantly and was thrilled that it was under a foot or so of earth. This was one of Jemma's favorite games; find the buried treasure. Grunting and rumbling, she dug with her sturdy forepaws, dirt flying everywhere.

Within thirty-seconds she had uncovered half of the body and the feet completely. She jerked at the shoe nearest her. What fun, she thought. The hill had never been as much fun as it had been for the past two days.

Mrs. Rappaport was stunned almost to paralysis of motion. Standing at her kitchen window, she strained her eyes looking through the binoculars in an effort to see why earth was being flung through the air in the bushes, right where she knew Mr. Rappaport to be. Her head began to ache, until she saw the dog come out from the brush into the small clearing, running in circles and tossing his shoe into the air.

"You disgusting little beast," Mrs. Rappaport said aloud, as her face contorted with anger. "There's only one solution for you. It's time for you to join Mr. Rappaport, you flea bitten canine. Tonight."

Jemma, meanwhile, was so elated she had found her quarry again, that chewing on the shoe became secondary. From her point of view, she had dug a hole, found her delicious, prized possession and, as an extra bonus, covered herself with dirt. She hadn't minded that she lost her pink bow, for she was a dog of great courage and strength.

A descendant of warriors that brought bulls to their knees, was our Jemma. She gave a heady flip to the shoe and it sailed through the air, landing almost twenty feet away. She was about to run after it when she heard her mistress's voice, a voice that brought Jemma back to the here and now. She grunted and ran down the hill to listen to an alarmed owner question the condition of her once clean and well-groomed dog. Jemma spent the better part of the day at the groomers, where she acquired a pert blue bow.

* * * *

Mrs. Rappaport had a new plan. She knew the dog's name. She also knew the dog came to the plateau twice a day, mornings and evenings.

She decided against using the pistol, as she had almost done in her panic the day before. That was too noisy and might make the dog's owners climb up the hill before she had time to return to her house. The shovel was too cumbersome and hard to manage; she had learned that the hard way. She had been aiming for the dog's head but missed the animal's body completely. No, the shovel was out.

Her weapon of choice was a heavy, and deadly sledgehammer. She had seen her deceased husband use to knock down a wall between the bathroom and a closet several years ago. Yes, Mrs. Rappaport thought, practice swinging it in the garage, this will do very nicely. One smack of this and the dog will be silent forever.

* * * *

That evening the woman sat beside the half-buried body of her husband, extremely content to watch beetles and other bugs crawl all over him. She had not bothered to rebury him, as soon there would be another, smaller creature in the grave. She smiled at the thought.

Jemma almost didn't come to the park that night. She wasn't sure what was happening but whatever it was, it wasn't good. Her owners were having a discussion about the condition she'd returned in that morning and she sensed her female owner was opposed to the outing.

Finally, Jemma saw the male kiss the female on the forehead and turn to her. Fifteen minutes later than usual, man and dog were taking their customary evening walk. As the man tried to walk past the hill, Jemma wrenched the leash out of his hand and scurried up her well-worn path.

Leash dragging behind her and unheeding her master's calls, she stopped about ten feet away from the ever-ripening man, now sans shoes.

"Come here, Jemma. There's a good dog," Mrs. Rappaport said stepping out of the shadows, both hands behind her back, and smiling.

Jemma cocked her head. The woman's tone was insincere, so Jemma stood her ground.

"What have I got, Jemma?" the woman crooned, bringing one hand forward and waving a tasseled loafer. "Come and get it, you mangy mutt."

Fortunately, Jemma didn't understand the words 'mangy mutt' or she would have been highly insulted. She'd never had mange in her life. But she did notice the shoe in the woman's hand and focused her attention on it.

"Jemma!" called her master from down below.

The dog turned her head toward the sound of his voice, as the woman put one foot on the end of the leash. Jemma looked back at her. Mrs. Rappaport stepped closer and closer on the leash, dangle the shoe enticingly in front of her.

"Jemma, come on, baby. Come on down now."

Jemma turned her head again to her master's voice and the woman brought the other hand forward containing the lethal sledgehammer. Her arm slowly went up over her head in preparation for the fatal strike.

Jemma looked back at Mrs. Rappaport and came to attention. Another game! It's Throw the Toy Time. Jemma played this game countless times with her owners and knew that with her short, stubby legs, she should get a head start. As the woman's arm continued back, Jemma turned her body to face the other way and made a lunge forward.

At first she felt the weight of the woman standing on the leash but, ultimately, pulling one hundred and thirty pounds or so was a small handicap in the long, illustrious career of English bulldogs. They were built, not for speed, but for power. Jemma's massive chest sucked in enough air to feed the mighty muscles in her upper torso and she leapt forward feeling the weight on the leash suddenly release.

Jemma ran for several feet and then turned back to make sure she was heading in the right direction of the thrown toy. What she saw baffled her enough to make her not even hear her master's pressing calls.

For there was the woman, lying on the ground, with her head resting on a rock. Jemma's eyes were drawn toward the movement directly over the woman's head. She saw the toy rotating, going up, up into the sky until it paused and then began its revolving descent back down, where the heavy steel hit the woman in the dead center of her forehead. Jemma heard a slight crack and then silence, broken only by her master's voice.

"Jemma Marie, don't make me come up there after you!"

Now Jemma knew that when she was called Jemma Marie, she'd better hustle and hustle she did. She ran to where the woman dropped the shoe, not bothering to look at the sightless eyes staring up at the darkening sky. Jemma grabbed the shoe by the tassel and ran down the hill.

"Jemma, it's about time. What have you got there, Girl? What is it? Give it to Daddy. There's a good girl, give it to Daddy."

Books by Heather Haven

The Alvarez Family Murder Mysteries
Murder is a Family Business, Book 1
A Wedding to Die For, Book 2
Death Runs in the Family, Book 3
DEAD...If Only, Book 4
The CEO Came DOA, Book 5
The Culinary Art of Murder, Book 6

The Lee Alvarez Mystery Novelettes
Honeymoons Can Be Murder, Book 1
Marriage Can Be Murder, Book 2 (October 2017)

The Persephone Cole Vintage Mysteries
The Dagger Before Me, Book 1
Iced Diamonds, Book 2
The Chocolate Kiss-Off, Book 3

Noir Mystery Stand Alone
Death of a Clown

Collection of Short Stories
Corliss and Other Award-Winning Stories

Multi-Author Boxed Sets
Sleuthing Women: 10 First-in-Series Mysteries
Sleuthing Women II: 10 Mystery Novellas

About Heather Haven

After studying drama at the University of Miami in Miami, Florida, Heather went to Manhattan to pursue a career. There she wrote short stories, novels, comedy acts, television treatments, ad copy, commercials, and two one-act plays, produced at several places, such as Playwrights Horizon. Once she even ghostwrote a book on how to run an employment agency. She was unemployed at the time.

One of her first paying jobs was writing a love story for a book published by Bantam called *Moments of Love*. She had a deadline of one week but promptly came down with the flu. Heather wrote "The Sands of Time" with a raging temperature, and delivered some pretty hot stuff because of it. Her stint at New York City's No Soap Radio - where she wrote comedic ad copy – help develop her long-time love affair with comedy.

She has won five awards so far for the humorous Alvarez Family Murder Mysteries. The Persephone Cole Vintage Mysteries and *Corliss and Other Award Winning Stories* have garnered several, as well.

However, her proudest achievement is winning the Independent Publisher Book Awards (IPPY) 2014 Silver Medal for her stand-alone noir mystery, **Death of a Clown**. As the real-life daughter of Ringling Brothers and Barnum and Bailey circus folk, she was inspired by stories told throughout her childhood by her mother, a trapeze artist and performer. The book cover even has a picture of her mother sitting atop an elephant from that time. Her father trained the elephants. Heather brings the daily existence of the Big Top to life during World War II, embellished by her own murderous imagination.

Connect with Heather at the following sites:

Website: **www:heatherhavenstories.com**
Heather's Blog:
 http://heatherhavenstories.com/blog/
https://www.facebook.com/HeatherHavenStories
https://www.twitter.com/Twitter@HeatherHaven

Sign up for Heather's newsletter at:
http://heatherhavenstories.com/subscribe-via-email/

Email: **heather@heatherhavenstories.com**.

I
     She'd love to hear from you. Thanks so much!

The Wives of Bath Press

The Wife of Bath was a woman of a certain
age, with opinions, who's on a journey.
Heather Haven and Baird Nuckolls are
modern day Wives of Bath.

www.thewivesofbath.com